Once Upon A Time:

Twisted Sexy Fairy Tales

LACY JANE

LACY JANE

Once Upon a Time: Twisted Sexy Fairy Tales Volume 1 (Books 1-3)

Contents

Preface

Once upon a time, there were fairy tales. No. Not that kind. These are not fairy tales for children. These are very adult, twisted, sexy fairy tales to keep you warm at night. There will be several in this series. I hope you enjoy them.

Love,

Lacy

One

1

Goldie

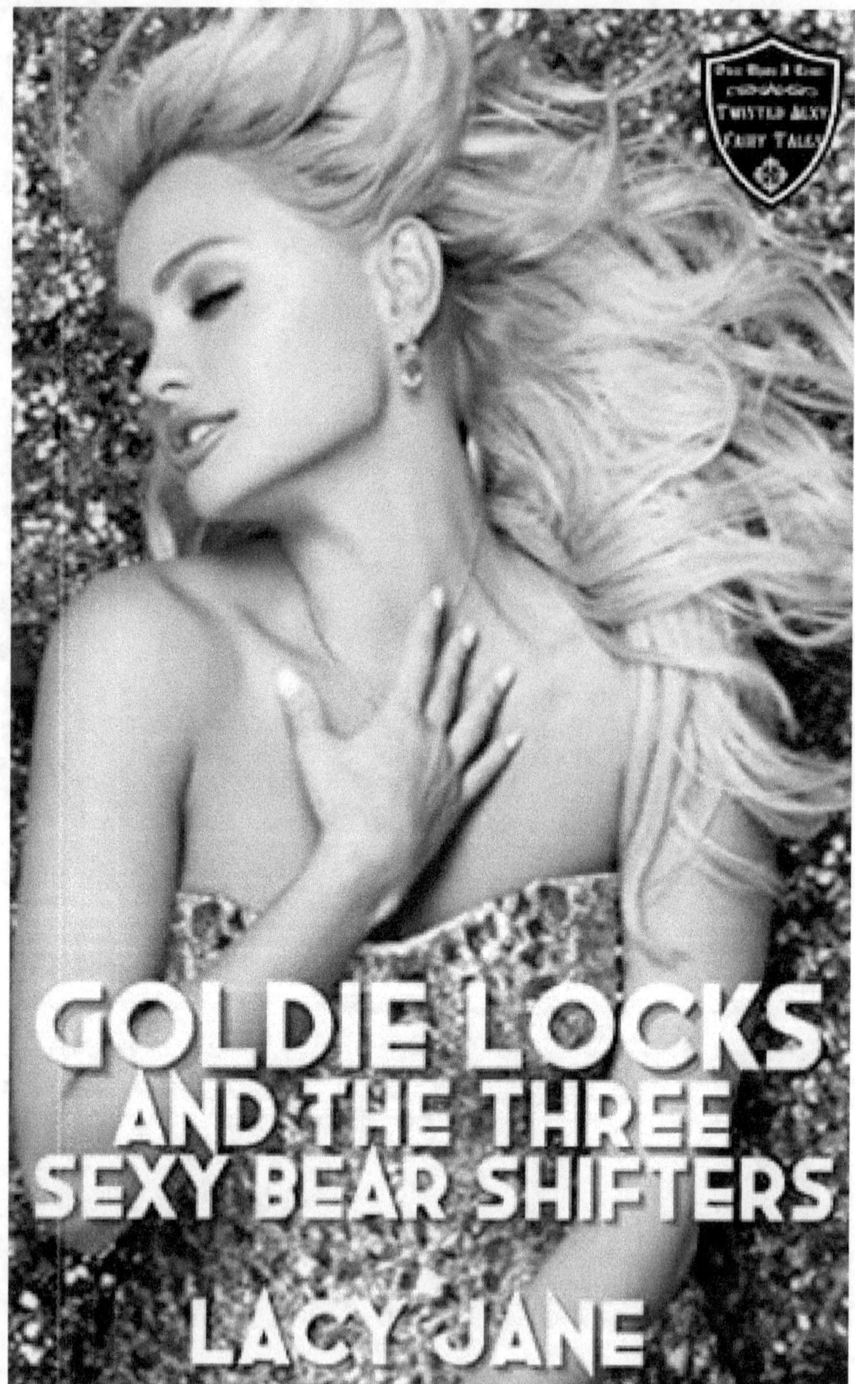
GOLDIE LOCKS
AND THE THREE
SEXY BEAR SHIFTERS
LACY JANE

Once upon a time, there was a girl named Goldie Locks, who had very naughty dreams...

I'm not like other girls my age. While they daydream about the captain of the football team or the cute boy in their math class, I daydream about three bear shifters. Actually, I daydream, nightdream, all the time dream, and am fucking obsessed with them.

The first time I dreamt of them, I had just turned thirteen...

There were three huge bears standing at the foot of a massive bed. They stared at me so strangely, almost like they were starving for me. It should have frightened me, but instead it made my tummy flutter.

I woke up longing to see the bears again. I have had tons of dreams about playing outside with them, laughing and feeling so happy. I have dreamt about them regularly over the years, but the dreams have happened more frequently and become much, much dirtier over the last few months.

I should introduce myself. I'm Goldie Locks. Seriously. My parents both have a really twisted sense of humor and thought it would be hilarious to name me Goldie. Now the joke is on them since I'm obsessed with three bears. Ha ha.

Since I turned eighteen last month, the dreams have become a nightly thing. They have gotten to the point that they take over the second I fall asleep. One of the dreams I have the most often, I had again last night…

I'm lying on a massive bed. The three men rush into the room in their bear forms. They stare at me as if they want to feast on me, but I know that they are not dangerous to me. They swiftly morph into the sexy men I've been dreaming about for years. Three men, so similar, yet so different.

They are all huge; at least six foot eight or nine. They have muscles upon muscles and are much broader than other men. Their hair is jet black, and their eyes are nearly black, too, with flecks of gold. They have neatly trimmed beards that I know will tickle when they kiss me. Their arms are massive, like they live in the gym, and their chests are ripped, too, with just enough hair to be sexy to the extreme. They each have that awesome vee that some men have that points down to their huge cocks. Wow. And yum. They are obviously brothers, but I can easily tell them apart despite the fact that they look so similar with their tan skin and dark hair.

I look down at their monstrous, hard cocks and feel moisture pool between my legs. They want me just as desperately as I want them. "Please," I beg them, writhing on the bed. They waste no time in ripping my clothes off of me. Instead of scaring me, their hunger just turns me on even more.

"Angel, we are your mates," the tallest of the three tells me while gently stroking my cheek. "We are going to mark you, pleasure you, and make you ours."

"Yes, please," I whisper. "Do whatever you want to me."

No sooner have I said that than the man takes my mouth in a ravenous kiss. He continues making love to my mouth while running his hands all over my body. I rub my hands up and down his chest before reaching for the hardness between his legs. It takes both of my hands to wrap around his girth. I give his cock a squeeze before working my hands down the length. Pre-cum is already spilling out, arousing me more. He pushes me down on the bed before sucking one nipple, then the other. It feels so good, but I need more. Then he puts his mouth against my pussy and devours it. He sucks on my clit, sending me spiraling. His beard is soaked with my juices. The other two get on either side of me, kissing my mouth, face, and neck before sucking my nipples and bringing my hands up to stroke both of their cocks.

So many mouths, hands, and cocks. All I feel is pleasure and the desperate need to be filled by them. I squirm under their ministrations; loving the sensations, but wanting so much more. They keep switching places so that everyone has a taste of my mouth, nipples, and pussy. Each of the men makes me come on their fingers and mouth. My screams of pleasure fill the room.

"We need to make you ours now," the sexy leader says while stroking his enormous cock.

"Yes, please!" I beg.

He moves over me and drives inside me with one hard thrust. I gasp at the sensation. It doesn't hurt as much as I had assumed it would. Instead, after a pinch of discomfort, I feel so much pleasure, it overwhelms me. With each thrust of his hips, I orgasm, soaking the bed with my cum. The others watch, waiting their turns and stroking their cocks.

"We are going to breed you tonight, sweetness," he whispers as he slams his cock into me again and again. As he lets go, he bites my nipple and pinches my clit. I scream as I orgasm again and feel him release stream after stream of cum into my hungry pussy. I know that he is right. These three incredibly virile men are going to get me pregnant tonight, and the thought amps up my desire even more.

He gives me a deep, passionate kiss before moving away from me. The second man takes his place. "Turn around, sweetheart. Up on all fours."

He kisses me gently before stroking my ass and pussy, working me into a frenzy with his fingers. I do as instructed and am rewarded with his cock filling me completely from behind. He pulls me against him and slams into me so hard, it almost hurts, but I want more. "Please don't hold back," I tell him. Apparently, that's all he needs to hear. He lifts me up and slams into me, again and again. As with his brother, my orgasms bleed into each other until I don't know where one ends and another begins. He holds me against him as he releases his cum inside me.

I am worn out, but I know the last man is still waiting for me, and I want him just as desperately as I wanted the other two. He motions for me to stand. I gasp as he picks me up like a rag doll and starts fucking me standing up, impaling me on his hard cock again and again until I'm running out of breath. I come continuously as he slams me down onto his cock over and over again. He releases inside me and gently lowers me to the bed. I'm surrounded by the three of them. They each reveal their sharp teeth, and lower them to my body; biting me at the same time. The ecstasy rolls through me so strongly, I pass out.

So, you see what I mean? Seriously, how is a wimpy little teenage boy going to compare to my three sexy bear shifters? Every time I dream about them, I wake up extremely horny and dripping from orgasms. All I can think about is having their hard cocks inside of me.

I've told my parents about my dreams. Well, not the specifics, but they pretty much get the gist. They are very open minded, and, frankly, don't seem as disturbed by the whole idea as you would think. That's why they are supporting my coming here today. I had a different dream last night; well, more like a flash. It showed a sign that said Landry National Park, so that's where I am now. It's a few hours from my house in Lambert, Colorado, but I feel like I'm supposed to be here. So I'm here. Hiking. Not my thing at all, but it really is beautiful here. I've seen some wild animals-deer, squirrels, and even a fox, but no bears yet. Are my shifters here? I really hope so. You have no idea how badly I want to meet and (let's be real) fuck my very sexy mates. I feel like I am getting closer to finding them.

I take a moment to appreciate the beauty surrounding me. This forest really is breathtaking. I don't think I've been anywhere so lovely before. I'm surrounded by mountains. It somehow makes me feel a sense of peace I've never felt anyplace else.

I've only been walking for a couple of hours, but I'm suddenly exhausted. I see smoke through the trees. I walk into a clearing and see the most perfect log cabin imaginable. Its wrap around porch and rocking chairs look so inviting. "It's stunning," I breathe reverently. Maybe the people inside will take pity on me, and let me lie down and take a nap. I knock on the door several times, but no one answers. "Hello?" I say, trying the doorknob. It's unlocked. I walk in and find that the cabin is even more impressive on the inside. The soaring wood ceilings are probably twenty feet tall. The cabin is almost all one massive room with a chef's kitchen, spacious living room, and the biggest bed I've ever seen. There's something vaguely familiar about it, but I'm too tired to think about what it might be. I try it out. It is the softest, most comfortable mattress I have ever felt. It feels like I'm lying on a fluffy cloud. I smile and fall immediately into a deep slumber.

Two

Jonah

Shifters sometimes dream of their mates before meeting them. This is definitely true for my brothers and me. The dreams have gone on for years now. Just glimpses of our angel at first, then full on fuck fests. The three of us have known for a long time now that we would be sharing a mate. It was a little shocking at first, but we have come to terms with it. John, Jake, and I are triplets, after all, and are way closer than most brothers. We even share a massive bed. We live together, work together, and hang out together. We are as close as any brothers could possibly be; plus we have the whole shifter thing going on.

A lot of people don't even realize that shifters are real. They think they are just something in romance novels. Surprise! We do exist. Anyway. We keep to ourselves, in general. We live in a cabin in the mountains, pretty far from everyone. We make sure to only shift into our bear forms when no one else is around. We are pretty isolated, so that's really not a problem. We are miles from the nearest neighbor. We have to be careful, though. You never know what crazy ideas someone might get about us. We have heard horror stories about shifters even being experimented on. That's why it's always a good idea to stay under the radar.

In case you don't know, there is only one fated mate for each shifter. Well, in this case, a shared mate. Anyway, that mate is the only one the shifter will ever feel desire or love for. Shifters mate for life. End of story.

We all started dreaming about our angel at the same time. The last few months, though, we have been dreaming about her nonstop. She looks very young and beautiful with her golden hair, pale skin, and baby blue eyes. I'm assuming by the incredibly curvy body she has, that she is of age now and we will be able to find her soon.

We've gone into town some, and even gone to neighboring towns as well, hoping to pick up her scent. Nothing. Damn, I really hope we find her before long. The three of us are starting to get really grumpy. It's tough seeing your mate every night in your dreams, but not being able to touch her in real life.

We are not too far from the cabin, chopping up downed trees for firewood, when an incredibly delicious scent hits us. The three of us go completely still with shock. "It's gotta be her, right?" John asks.

"I'd say so. Let's find out."

We quickly shift into our bear forms and race toward the amazing scent of our beautiful, perfect mate.

Three

Goldie

I'm dreaming again. Obviously. I look up and see the three bears. They are gigantic. A normal person would be scared to death, but not me. I live for these dreams where I see my mates. I know my bears would never hurt me. They shift into their human forms.

My lord, they are hot. "Oh my god. You are all so gorgeous," I say, looking at my very sexy mates. I am suddenly so turned on that I can't think straight. I rub my clit, which is absolutely drenched. My panties are ruined. I look up to see my three ravenous men looking like they plan to eat me for dinner.

"Angel, you are our mate," the first man growls while staring at me. His voice sends shivers down my spine. "You belong to us." The others nod in agreement.

"Yes!" I rush to agree. "I am yours. Please do whatever you want to me," I say, while fingering my pussy and lifting my hips off the bed in invitation. I hear growls from all three of them, and look up to see each of them stroking their massive cocks. I scream as an orgasm hits me hard.

Suddenly, the men are everywhere. They are dragging my shoes off, and immediately pull my pants and panties off after. They tear my shirt off, sending buttons flying, then undo my bra and throw it across the room. Damn, this dream really feels real. At least, that's what I assume until one of the men puts his mouth on my pussy and I gush all over his face.

"Oh my gosh. I'm not dreaming. Am I?" I manage to ask.

"No, sunshine. You are not dreaming. This is real. We have been dreaming about you for years now, and you are finally here. You have no idea how hungry we are for you."

"Well, then. Why don't you show me? Fuck me, mate."

Four

Jonah

Jesus. Our angel is the sexiest thing I've ever laid eyes on. I know my brothers feel the same. We have been dreaming about her for so long. I can't believe she is actually here. We rip the rest of her clothes off her sexy body. I would be worried about scaring her, but our girl is totally on board. When she came on my face, it took everything I had not to come right then. The only place I'm putting my seed is where it belongs; inside my mate's sweet cunt.

I lick her delicious honey hole again and again; fucking her with my tongue. I use my fingers to help loosen her up. She will be taking three giant bear shifters, and we aren't exactly known for being gentle; especially when we find our mate. I suck her clit hard, causing her to come again.

We each take turns kissing her pouty pink lips and licking and sucking every inch of her beautiful body. Her pale skin is the softest I've ever touched; like a baby's skin. She's short, but has incredible curves. She is perfect for fucking and breeding. She looks like a sexy centerfold with her long blond hair spread out behind her, and her bare pussy glistening. Her heavy tits are the most incredible things I've ever seen. I take my time sucking and biting her rosy little nipples, while my brothers take turns licking her honey pot.

She is writhing on the bed, primed and ready for us. Her vanilla scent mixed with her arousal is driving me insane.

"Open up, sweetness. It's time to fuck your mates."

Five

Goldie

"Yes!" I scream. I've never needed anything so badly in my entire life. My pussy feels so empty. It longs to be rammed with the gigantic hard cocks my mates are sporting. I spread my legs eagerly; ready to be filled.

The first man lines his cock up to my drenched hole and slams himself inside. I scream, both with a stab of pain and the most pleasure I've ever experienced. My fingernails are probably drawing blood as they dig into his back. He gives me a few seconds to get used to his size before he pulls back and slams in again. He does this a few times until I have every bit of his giant cock inside of me. I can hear his ragged breathing, along with that of my other mates.

"I'll try to be gentle, little one, but it's not going to be easy for me." I look into his beautiful eyes and inhale his manly scent. These men all smell amazing; like leather, outdoors, and men. Big, strong, burly, sexy men.

"Please don't be gentle," I say breathlessly. "I need to be taken hard by all three of you."

The men groan in unison before the man starts pounding into my pussy so hard that the headboard is slamming against the wall. Orgasm after orgasm burst from me so strong that I'm afraid I might pass out. He lifts my legs over his arms and pounds into me even deeper.

"You love me fucking the hell out of your sweet little cunt, don't you, Angel?"

"Yes!" I scream as another orgasm wracks my body.

"We're going to breed you!" he screams as he presses his finger against my clit hard, making me come again.

"Yes!" I scream, raking my nails down his back as I take rope after rope of his seed inside my greedy cunt.

Six

Jake

"My turn," I growl, practically knocking Jonah out of the way. Our girl has just been thoroughly fucked, but I can't give her time to recover. I've waited thirty-five years to find my mate. I could have eaten her sweet pussy all day long. I'm already addicted to the taste and scent of her. I'm not about to wait another second to be inside her.

"On your hands and knees, baby." I kiss her lips and neck before flipping her over and slamming myself to the hilt inside her warm, wet hole. "Fuck!" I yell. "Your sweet little pussy is choking the life out of my cock."

Damn. The wetness dripping from her tells me she likes it when I talk nasty. "You like me talking dirty to you?" I ask as I pump into her harder.

"Yes," she answers breathlessly.

"Damn, that's hot. Beg me to fuck you, baby."

"Please fuck me harder! I need your cock!"

I rare back and plow into her with everything I've got. I pinch her hard little nipples while I fuck her. My brother is right. We are definitely getting our girl pregnant tonight. Just the thought of her belly round with our baby sends me over the edge, making me spill my load inside her beautiful body.

Seven

John

"I need you, too," our angel says once my brother finishes with her.

"About fucking time," I growl, picking her up and impaling her on my giant cock in one move, making her scream. I groan. She feels even better than I had imagined. "Jesus. You feel incredible. I'm sorry to be so rough with you, angel. I just want you too much to go slow."

"Don't worry. I don't want you to go slow. I like it hard and rough."

Damn. She is perfect. I fuck her even harder. Her hot little cunt is squeezing the hell out of my cock. Every time she comes, her pussy squeezes me tighter. I pound into her like my very own fuck toy, and she loves every minute of it. I've never heard sexier sounds in my life than the cries and screams our girl makes while she's being fucked by one of us.

I hold out as long as possible, but our sexy girl is too much. Watching her ripe tits bounce in front of my face as I fuck her tests my control. Before long, her tight as hell pussy finally milks all the cum from my body.

I roll off of her and give her a few minutes to rest and recoup. I look at my brothers, who both nod at me. We have to explain what's about to happen. "We all have to bite you at the same time to finish the mating ritual, sweetheart," I say gently, while stroking her cheek. The three of us are nervous about her reaction. Most humans freak out when they hear something like that, but not our angel. She is perfect for us in every way.

"I know," she says calmly. "Finish making me yours."

We take turns kissing her hungrily, before piercing her skin with our sharp teeth. The pleasure is so intense, the four of us orgasm hard and pass out.

Eight

Goldie

"Best. Dream. Ever," I mumble as I start to wake up. When I try to roll over, though, I find I can't move. As I shift my legs, the ache between them tells me that last night really happened. I open my eyes and see all three of my mates in bed with me, in all their naked glory. Finally! Instead of waking up alone and horny, I am waking up with the three hottest men I've ever seen. Definitely still horny, though. I think they can help me with that. Damn, but my mates are fine! I rake my eyes down their sexy, naked bodies. Every inch of them makes me hot. No wonder no one else has ever interested me. No one else could possibly compare.

The three of them wake at once, and stare hungrily at me. As sore as it is, my pussy aches, wanting more of the three men. They start stroking their hands up and down my body; my arms, my legs, my breasts. I ache everywhere. I am shocked to see their cocks completely hard again. "Oh, my," I breathe, excited to see what else they have in store for me. They take turns kissing me for several minutes before stopping to talk to me.

Nine

Jonah

As much as I want our angel again, I know we should at least spend some time getting to know her first. We need to treat our mate with love and respect, but it's really tough when your dick is doing all the thinking for you.

"Sweetheart, before we take you again, we should probably introduce ourselves. I'm Jonah Bear. These are my brothers, Jake and John."

"Hi. I'm Goldie. Goldie Locks."

We all burst out laughing. "Seriously, sweetheart. What's your name?"

"I promise you, Jonah, I am not even kidding. That is actually my name."

He smiles. "I suppose it's pretty appropriate, considering."

She smiles and nods. "Is Bear seriously your last name?"

"Yes, baby. It is. And it will be added to your name as soon as possible."

"That sounds wonderful, but I think I need to spend a little more time in bed with my mates first. Don't you? I have an ache right here," I say, dipping my fingers in my dripping wet cunt. "You three are the only ones who can make it better."

We all growl and jump on our gorgeous mate. We'll have to leave this cabin at some point, but it definitely won't be today. I push her down and have my mouth on her cunt before she knows what hit her. Damn, I could lick her honey all day long, but my cock needs his turn, too. I pull her on top of me and watch her impale herself on my dick.

"Fuck!" we both cry at the same time. Watching her fuck me is so sexy. Her sweet pussy is squeezing my cock like a vise. Her heavy tits bounce in front of my face. I squeeze them hard, then take turns sucking and biting her hard nipples. She really likes it when I'm a little rough with them. She looks like a goddess as she rides me. She starts rocking faster until I finally have to take over. I lay her down on the bed, put her legs over my arms and pound the hell out of her sweet cunt. She screams out as she comes again and milks my release out of me.

Ten

Jake

"Brother, you gotta share," I say as gently as I can. Jonah gives Goldie a sweet kiss, then rolls off to the other side of the bed to recover. My mate is laid out before me like the finest feast, and I can't wait to sample everything on the menu.

"Come here, sweetheart," I motion for her to come to the edge of the bed. "I need to feel your sweet mouth wrapped around my cock." She licks her puffy lips hungrily, then devours half of my cock on the first try.

"Damn, baby. That feels so good." She gags a little as she tries to take too much. "You don't need to take it all, sweetness. We'll love anything you do to us."

She pulls back and starts licking the head of my cock like a lollipop. She scoops out some pre-cum with her tongue and swallows it. "Mmmm. Delicious."

I need to come, but every bit is going inside of her ripe pussy. I toss her on the bed and fuck her like the animal I am. I have no control when it comes to her. I can't get enough. I slam my cock inside her again and again, loving the noises she makes and the cum that drips from her sweet little hole. The sound of my cock going in and out of her is loud in the quiet room. She screams out and her cunt grips my cock so hard, I can't hold out any longer. I come so hard, I black out.

Eleven

John

"Come here, sweetheart. Ride my cock."

Goldie smiles as she lowers herself onto my throbbing dick. Damn. She feels so good. It takes everything I have not to come immediately. Her warm heat grips me as she slams herself down on my cock, harder and harder.

"Help me," she says. I know what she needs. Our girl likes it really hard. I grip her shoulders, pushing her down even harder, until I feel her cervix against my dick.

"Yes!" she screams. I slam her down on my cock faster and faster, loving the feel of liquid gushing from her. Finally, I let go and come hard in her sweet, addictive pussy.

Twelve

Goldie

After spending a glorious morning in bed, we decide to go outside into the beautiful forest. My mates introduce me to their bears. They are three giant grizzlies, who look terrifying, but are total teddy bears with me. They vie for my attention like little children. Each pushes their head against my hand, wanting to be petted like a dog. They take turns licking my face, sending me into a fit of giggles. After that, they let me ride on their backs while they run around. I feel so free and happy with my mates.

They cook me a delicious dinner of steak and vegetables. I sit and watch them preparing the meal since they won't let me do anything. They treat me like a queen.

I have learned so much about them today. They sell firewood and make custom wood furniture. It's all very impressive. They even built their gorgeous cabin themselves.

They only go into town once a month or so for supplies. They have a massive extra refrigerator and freezer in the garage so that they have plenty of food in case of a snowstorm. They have a backup generator, too. They are pretty self sufficient, for the most part. There's enough food here to sustain them for several months.

After dinner, we spend the rest of the evening outside running around again before finally collapsing. Today has been filled with lots of sex and getting to know each other. We are all exhausted. We need to get a good night's sleep tonight, though. After all, tomorrow is a big day. I am taking my mates to meet my parents.

Thirteen

John

Today, we are on our way to meet Goldie's parents. She's our mate no matter what, but it would be nice if her parents could like and accept us.

She looks over at me. "Don't look so worried. My parents have known for years that I would be mated to the three of you. I know it sounds nuts, but they are very accepting. They just want me to be happy."

"That's what we want, too, baby."

"The three of you make me very happy."

I pull her into my lap for a kiss. But the longer I kiss her, the more I want. So does she. Before I know it, she is grinding her sweet little pussy against me, and I can't hold back anymore. Her dress provides easy access. I push it up, rip the soaked panties from her body, and release my steel rod from the denim prison he is in. There's no time for finesse. I lay her down on the backseat and push all the way inside her drenched cunt. I nearly come just from hearing her moans of pleasure.

"What the fuck?" Jonah says.

"Hey, man! This has to be equal," Jake chimes in.

"Brother, you are so right," Jonah slaps him on the shoulder, and turns off of the highway.

We pull onto a dirt road, but I couldn't care less. I'm fucking my woman so hard I'm seeing stars. I finally come inside her and collapse. After a few seconds, I am lifted off of her.

"My turn," growls Jonah.

Fourteen

Jonah

It took everything I had to not pull over and fuck Goldie before, but when John started screwing her, there was no way in hell I was waiting any longer. She looks at me and smiles. I kiss her soft lips and squeeze her juicy tits. I can't wait to see them filled with milk. Just the thought of it makes me even harder. "I can't take it slow, Goldie."

"Good. I don't want you to. Fuck me as hard as you want, Jonah."

I shed my clothes and plow inside her sweet cunt. "Fuck, sweet pea. I could do this all day."

"Me, too," she moans. I devour her mouth and tits while I fuck her, never letting up. Her cries get louder and louder.

"You love it when I fuck you hard, don't you?" I breathe against her ear.

"Yes! I love it! I love when you fuck me. I love all three of you."

That's enough to milk every drop of cum from my body. I pull her against me; raining kisses on her face and giving her a minute to rest before Jake takes over.

Fifteen

Jake

It's my turn to have our sweet mate. We aren't going to make it to her parents' house today because we had to have her again. I punch my hips forward and pound her sweet, sweet pussy. She nips my ear and bites my neck, sending me into overdrive.

"You're my dirty little girl, aren't you?"

"Yes, I'm your dirty girl. Fuck me hard, Jake."

"You love your mates' giant cocks, don't you?"

"Yes!" she screams, while I pound her pussy mercilessly. "Put your baby in me." Her sexy words are enough to push me over the edge.

Darkness consumes me as I fall into the deepest sleep of my life.

Sixteen

Goldie

We all ended up sleeping in the truck last night. You would think it would be horribly uncomfortable, but it really wasn't. Even though my men are ridiculously muscular, they are really comfy to sleep on. Not to mention, we were all really worn out.

I had let my mom know we would be coming by today. She didn't sound too surprised. She had assumed I would find my mates. I just hope everything goes well.

"It will be fine," Jonah whispers in my ear.

"Are you a mind reader?"

"Just with you. Now that we are mated, we can read each other's thoughts."

"Seriously? Huh. I didn't know that."

"There's a lot you don't know, but we will teach you."

"I'd really like that," I say, giving his hand a squeeze.

Seventeen

Jonah

"See. What did I tell you?" I say to her mentally.

"This is so weird," she sends back.

Joe and Beth Locks, Goldie's parents, are as nice as they can be. Beth looks like an older, tinier version of our beautiful mate, while Joe is tall with salt and pepper hair and our angel's blinding smile. I really expected judgment or anger from the two of them, but all they show us is love and acceptance. They know a few mated couples, so they know how it works; although our situation is a bit different. I can feel the relief flowing from Goldie that everything is going so well. I ask for their permission to marry their daughter. Even though technically she will be married to me, in reality, she will be married to the three of us. It's very important to all of us. My brothers and I want our mate tied to us in every way, so we need to marry her as soon as possible. Her parents give us their blessing, and we all have a nice dinner to celebrate.

My brothers and I would like to marry Goldie today, but we know this is the one and only wedding for us and our angel. We finally agree that we will wait a week so that she can have everything she wants for her wedding day. We would do anything to make Goldie happy.

Eighteen

Goldie

A week later…

It's my wedding day. We are having a very private ceremony. Just me and my mates, my parents, and my soon to be in-laws, who are really wonderful. I got to meet them a few days ago. I was so nervous, but they are awesome. I love them and they love me. They aren't weirded out by our situation, thank god. They seem very excited about the possibility of having grandkids sometime soon.

Mom and I have rushed around all week, gotten everything together for the wedding, and even found the perfect dress. It's a gorgeous, strapless gown with little jewels all over it. The stones form what look like little bear paws. I kid you not. When I saw it, I knew it was the perfect dress to marry my bear shifters in.

The Wedding March starts playing, and I take my father's arm. He walks me down the aisle to my three sexy mates. Their eyes are filled with happiness and hunger, much like mine probably are. I say my vows to each of them and them to me. They place a stunning diamond on my finger, with a matching wedding band. I put a ring on each of them. I am so thankful I wore waterproof makeup as I feel tears of happiness run down my face. We are finally pronounced men and wife. We now belong to each other in every way. Each man kisses me tenderly.

"I love you all so much."

"We love you, too," they each say. They each start telling me mentally all the things they plan to do to me tonight, making me blush and drench my panties. I shift my legs, trying and failing to get some relief. I can't wait to get back to the cabin with them.

Nineteen

Goldie

We make it back home in record time. When we walk inside, I am stunned. My husbands have managed to decorate the cabin with fairy lights everywhere. It looks beautiful. The whole room glows, illuminating the many flowers adorning every surface; including the rose petals decorating the bed.

"Oh, my gosh. This is gorgeous! You guys are so good to me," I say as I hug each of my men.

"We love our beautiful mate. We just want you to be happy," Jonah says, smiling. The others nod their heads in agreement.

"I've never been so happy before," I tell them while strolling casually to the bed. "You could make me even happier, though. You know, our marriage hasn't been consummated yet." That's all it takes for my three men to surround me, kissing my lips and neck, while trying to undo all of the tiny buttons on my dress. Their giant fingers are having difficulty performing that task. I can feel desire rolling off of them. Their arousal makes mine burn that much hotter.

"Just rip it," I say heatedly. Jake rips my dress down the back. The next thing I know, my men are devouring me from head to toe. "Should we try something new?" I ask them.

"Like what?" John asks.

"Taking all three of you at once?" They each growl and their cocks seem to get even harder.

"Are you sure about this, sweetheart?" Jonah asks.

"Yes. I want every part of me to belong to the three of you."

Each of the men strip quickly. They silently agree on positions. Jonah lies down on the bed, pulling me on top of him. It only takes me a couple of tries to get his cock all the way inside of my hungry pussy. Jake gets behind me, sliding one finger, then two into my puckered hole. It feels strange, but arousing. Soon, he starts pushing inside me with the head of his cock. "Oh my god!" I scream with pleasure. He manages to push all the way in.

"Me, too, angel," John says, while pushing his angry looking cock into my mouth. I take him deeper and deeper, trying not to gag. I swallow and feel his cock hitting the back of my throat. The three of them pump into me at the same time, drawing orgasm after orgasm out of my well used body. Their grunts are such a turn on. Before long, they all lose control, fucking me harder and harder until they explode inside me, triggering an intense orgasm that makes me quiver from head to toe.

"Wow," I say breathlessly.

"Wow is right," my three men say simultaneously.

"Are you okay?" Jonah asks.

"Never better," I reply, giving each of my men a passionate kiss. Jonah picks me up and carries me into the enormous shower. They take turns washing me off as I wash them. After a while, we dry off and crash for the night. Our wedding day has been perfect.

Twenty

Epilogue 1-Jonah

A month later…

I walk inside the cabin and find my wife bawling. "What's wrong, baby? What happened?"

She tries to tell me, but she's crying so hard, she doesn't make any sense. "Wedonthaveanyicecream."

"Huh? Sweetheart. Calm down for a second. Concentrate and tell me with your mind."

"We don't have any mint chocolate chip ice cream!" she screams in my head.

"It's okay, baby. We'll get you some." I call John and have him make an emergency trip to the grocery store. I don't know why this is so urgent, but I've never seen Goldie so upset. I wrap my arms around her and rock her from side to side until she calms down.

****

A short while later, John and Jake rush in with a year's supply of ice cream. Believe me, the three of us spoil the shit out of our mate every chance we get. She spies the ice cream and practically knocks us down to get to it. She grabs a spoon and scarfs down one of the pints in record time.

The three of us exchange worried glances. "Do you think she has a tapeworm?" Jake whispers. I shake my head. I'm not sure what is wrong with our mate, but she is all out of sorts.

"Thank you!" she says as she gives us each an extra long hug and kiss. Her arousal fills my nose and turns my dick to stone. "Mmm. You all smell so good," she says, while stroking our chests. "I need to feel you. Now," she says, stripping off her dress to reveal her perfect, naked body underneath. The three of us growl and waste no time shucking our clothes and satisfying our mate's craving for our cocks.
****

Later, I'm wrapped around Goldie, squeezing her luscious tits. "Damn, you are so sensitive, baby." She has come twice just from me pinching her nipples. It finally dawns on me. I sniff her cunt like the animal I am.

"What are you doing, Jonah?" she giggles.

"I'm smelling your sweet cunt that smells even sweeter than normal. You're pregnant, angel."

"What?" the three of them shout at once.

"Of course!" Jake and John agree, but our mate just looks confused.

"Sweetheart, think about it. You've been fucked countless times by three very virile shifters with no protection. You've been emotional. You've cried at several commercials. You thought the world was coming to an end when you didn't have ice cream. Your tits are super sensitive. Baby, you've got a shifter cub growing inside you."

I see the moment realization hits her. "Oh my God!" she touches her stomach reverently. "We're having a baby!" Tears of happiness stream down her face. She hugs each of us before we claim her again like the ravenous beasts we are.

Twenty-One

Epilogue 2-Goldie

Five years later…

I hear giggles as my three little bear cubs play hide and seek with their fathers. That's right. Just like my husbands, my babies are nearly identical triplets-Jackson, Jagger, and Julian. My hubbies wanted to stick with the J names. I had a really rough delivery with three giant shifter babies, so we decided to stop at three.

My parents are visiting for the weekend. I am so excited because I know I will get some quality alone time with my men tonight, because my parents are always happy to spend extra time with their grandbabies. They are awesome that way. Even after five years, I can't wait to be alone with my sexy mates. We still want each other just as much as that first time. I guess that's what happens when you are mated to three sexy shifters. Lucky me!

Our babies just started shifting recently, and it is just freaking adorable. I watch as my parents try to hold in their laughter at them. They are hiding behind a pole that is about three inches wide. They don't yet get that we can still see them. My three big bears find them and hold them down, tickling them. Their laughter echoes through the mountain. My heart is overflowing. The six of them are my everything.

Goldie Locks, the three bear shifters, and their three baby bears lived happily ever after.

THE END

Twenty-Two

Chapter 22

Once Upon A Time:
TWISTED SEXY
FAIRY TALES
LITTLE RED
AND THE
BIG, BAD,
SEXY WOLF
LACY JANE

49

Twenty-Three

Scarlett

Once upon a time, there was a girl named Scarlett. She was on her way to her grandma's house, not knowing that she was about to meet a big, bad, sexy wolf.

I am driving up the steep mountain road to meet Granny's realtor at her house. Granny took a vacation to Miami last month and loved it so much, she decided to move there. She came home, packed everything up, and was on her way. Which brings me to now. She asked me to show her house to Mr. Wolf, the realtor she randomly chose. After everything Granny has done for me, it's really the least that I can do. Considering she raised me as her own after my folks took off for parts unknown right after I was born, I kind of owe her. She is pretty much the only parent I have had for all of my twenty-two years. Granny is my favorite person in the world. I miss her already. I don't mind helping her out; really, I don't. My Mini Cooper just wasn't made for these steep mountain roads.

When I finally make it to Granny's cabin, I see that someone is already there, waiting on the front porch. I get out of my car, but when the man turns around to face me, I freeze. He is a behemoth of a man; well over six feet tall. He has sun kissed skin with short black hair, and a sexy beard I'd love to run my fingers through . He is wearing a suit that surely had to be custom made to fit his massive shoulders and chest. His eyes are a really odd amber color. They almost look like they are glowing.

The man is drop dead gorgeous, but it's not just that. I have never had any kind of attraction to anyone before, but this man is doing it for me in spades. I take a few steps toward him, and he makes an odd noise. Did he just growl at me?

Moisture pools between my legs. Damn. That has seriously never happened to me before. He takes a whiff of the air and suddenly looks ravenous. There is no way that he can know I'm wet. Right? I try to discreetly rub my legs together to get some relief, but it doesn't seem to help the ache any. I attempt to regain my composure, and approach him with an outstretched hand. "Hi. I'm Scarlett Jones; Daisy's granddaughter," I manage to squeak out.

He licks his lips. "I'm Damian Wolf," he says in his very husky voice. "Everyone just calls me Wolf, but you should call me Damian," he says, running his fingers down my neck, giving me goosebumps all over, and making my panties spontaneously combust. "I guess that makes you little red, and me, the big, bad wolf." He stares at me for so long, I feel like I'm in a trance. Instead of shaking my hand, he lifts it to his lips for a kiss. Shock waves roll through me and set every nerve in my body on fire. He spreads kisses across the top of my hand, shooting desire through my system and making me breathless. He tugs me closer, putting his mouth against my ear, and making it seem very warm outside despite the dropping temperature. "You might not realize it yet, but sweetheart? You. Are. Mine."

I don't think I can say no to this man. I don't even want to. I am so fucked.

Twenty-Four

Damian

Scarlett takes a deep breath and giggles nervously. She might think I'm kidding, but I'm not. I've been on this earth for forty-five years waiting for my fated mate. The second I looked at her, I was a goner. I couldn't have picked a more perfect match if I tried. She has pouty pink lips that I imagine wrapped around my cock, emerald green eyes that shine with merriment, and a cute dusting of freckles across her face. She has shiny ginger curls flowing to her waist, pale skin, and a curvy body just made to be fucked and bred. She will be able to handle the constant pounding I plan on giving her. She looks sweet and innocent, and I can't wait to dirty her up.

In case you don't know, wolves mate for life-not only normal wolves, but also wolf shifters, like myself. When a shifter finds his mate, her scent is intoxicating to him; the most delicious smell imaginable. I scoffed at that description before, thinking it was an exaggeration, but now I'm a believer. The second I caught a whiff of my gorgeous mate, I nearly stopped breathing. Now that I can smell her arousal, it is taking everything in me not to just throw her down and claim her. I'm having a really tough time holding back like I need to. I know that humans generally need more time than us to get used to the whole mate concept. I'm trying to give her a few minutes to catch up. I can't seem to keep my hands off of her, though. I breathe in her delicious scent, running my hand down the back of her neck.

Scarlett pulls away and shakily unlocks the front door, giving the first hint that I've rattled her. She has no idea at the restraint it is taking for me to not just throw her down on the floor and give her the hard fucking she deserves. She closes the door behind us and starts rattling off information about the cabin. I have a feeling that she talks nonstop when she is nervous.

I really don't give a shit about the listing anymore. From now on, all I care about is her-my perfect mate. My cock is standing at attention for the first time in my life. A wolf shifter can only be aroused by his or her mate, and let me tell you, my little red is arousing the hell out of me right now without even trying.

She nervously licks her lips, and my control is shot. I stalk toward her, hearing her shallow breaths. She is aroused by me, but nervous. She doesn't understand that she belongs to me now. The pull we feel toward each other is probably overwhelming for her.

I put my hand on the back of her neck, pulling her toward me. I kiss her lips gently, then her neck; licking the spot I will be biting very soon. Her pulse accelerates as she shifts her legs and pulls me closer. I can feel her nipples pebble against her bra. "Fuck, yes! You are mine. I need you, Scarlett. Now," I say, thrusting my hard cock against her.

Twenty-Five

Scarlett

What is happening to me? I was a normal girl up until a few minutes ago. Now I'm so turned on, I can't think straight. Since I set eyes on Damian, I can't think of anything but him. His touch sets me on fire.

"Has anyone else ever touched you like this, sweetheart?" he asks while stroking his hands up and down my body. I shake my head. I've never had any interest in anyone before. I'd never even been kissed until a few seconds ago. I don't understand why this man is making me feel so out of control. Sure, he's gorgeous, but it's more than that. I don't understand why I'm letting a man I just met seduce me. He grazes his fingertip over my engorged nipple before pinching it hard, causing me to orgasm.

"Oh, god! What am I doing?" I push him away from me, trying to regain my composure. Damn, he's hot. He could get any woman he wanted, and probably does. This is probably a common occurrence for him. I bet he uses his seductive powers on unsuspecting women every day. The thought pisses me off way more than it should.

"This is not a one time thing, sweetheart. We are made for each other. You are my fated mate. You are the only woman for me, and I am the only man for you. You are the woman I will spend my life with. The one I will kiss, touch, fuck every day, make babies with, and grow old with."

My heart is beating out of my chest. There's no way he's for real, right? People don't just set eyes on someone and know that it's their "one". Do they?

"Come here, Scarlett." He crooks his finger at me. He's like a force field, pulling me in. I feel hypnotized, unable to disobey his command, as I walk back to him.

"Good girl," he breathes against my ear, sending shivers down my spine and ruining my panties. He kisses my ear and neck gently, slowly making his way back around to my lips. His mouth barely touches mine, but electricity shoots through my entire body, awakening desires that I didn't even know I possessed. After a few seconds, the kiss becomes more urgent. His tongue tangles with mine. He picks me up like I weigh nothing, and holds me up against the wall while he takes my mouth over and over. He starts grinding his enormous hard cock against my pussy, causing me to explode again.

"Fuck, baby. You feel so good. I can't wait to be inside you." He pulls up my skirt, and rips my panties off. Damn. That is so hot! I should be outraged, but I am even more turned on than before. He slips his fingers inside my pussy lips, stroking me. I love feeling his hands and mouth on me. He pushes his fingers in harder, causing me to cry out again. He pulls them out and and licks my juices off of them like they are a delicacy. I am completely lost in the sensations he is sending through my body. "So responsive. So wet for me."

I'm ready to surrender until I look up and see his eyes glowing; like, literally glowing. It snaps me out of the spell I've been under. "What the fuck, Damian?" I push him away again. "What is wrong with your eyes?"

"My wolf is trying to break through and get to you. He's happy that we've found our mate."

Damn. He would have to be delusional. "Riiight. Your wolf. Okey dokey."

"You don't believe me."

"It doesn't matter what I believe."

"I only care about what you believe, sweetheart. Here, let me show you," he says, quickly shucking his clothes, and causing me to nearly hyperventilate.

"What are you doing?" I ask breathlessly, trying not to stare at his giant, muscular physique.

"I'm introducing you to my wolf."

Suddenly, his whole body contorts, and his bones make terrible popping noises. "Oh my god! What the hell?" Okay. So, apparently he isn't delusional after all. I am frozen in place as I take in the giant gray wolf now standing casually in Granny's cabin. I pinch myself to see if I'm dreaming. Nope. Not dreaming. I should be terrified, but I'm somehow soothed by the furry creature. He comes toward me, nudging me with his nose. I stroke his fur, causing him to purr noisily. I feel confident that he would never harm me.

"Is this seriously you?" He comes closer and licks my face, causing me to giggle again. If you would have told me a day ago that a wolf would lick my face and I would laugh about it, I would have thought you were stoned.

It only takes a few seconds for the wolf to morph back into the sexy man I met earlier. Only now, I can't help but notice his lack of clothing. It makes it really hard for me to pay attention to anything else. My eyes are fixated on the hard beast between his legs. I felt his cock against me earlier, but seeing it in all its glory? Whoa. It's enormous; so thick and long. It looks purple and angry, and is dripping cream from the tip. The ache between my legs intensifies. I am suddenly dying for a taste of Damian's giant cock. I try to look anywhere else, but I just can't help myself. I have never been so turned on.

He smiles at me like he can read what's going on in my dirty little mind. "You are welcome to explore me all you want, sweetheart, but I'm not sure you are ready for that yet. Would you feel more comfortable if I were dressed?"

"Definitely."

He quickly puts his clothes back on. "What do you know about shifters, baby?"

I know that this one is hot as fuck, but I don't say that. "Nothing, apparently. Up until a few minutes ago, I thought they were fictional."

"No. We are very real. There are a lot of us here, though we try to stay under the radar. When we find our fated mate, we mate for life. The first time I take you, I will mark you with my bite. That will complete our mating ritual, and let other shifters know that you are taken. There is only one fated mate for each shifter, and you are mine," he states as he kisses the side of my neck, making his way toward my aching breasts. I so badly want to just give in to my desire, giving us both what we want, but I need some space to clear my head first. That is the logical thing to do. Right?

I force myself to pull away. "I need some time," I say quietly. I see the disappointment on his face. I move further away, and feel like I'm missing a huge part of myself. Maybe this pull will go away when I'm not looking at his gorgeous face and body.

"I'm not happy about it, but I do understand. It's a lot for you to digest. Let me see your phone." I hand it over to him. "I'm programming my number in. I'll give you some time to come to terms with this. Call me when you are ready, or if you need anything. I will answer any questions you have. You can call me anytime, day or night, and I will be there."

"Okay," I say. I kiss him on the cheek, then flee like the hounds of Hell are after me.

Twenty-Six

Scarlett

"*My house. ASAP. Bring ice cream. 911,*" I text my bestie, Goldie. She is the only one I can think of to talk to about this. We met a few years ago when she moved to town to be with her husbands. Yes, husbands, plural. She has three. It sounds a little crazy, but the three giant brothers are obsessed with her and vice versa. There have been several times that I saw way more than I should have since her men can't seem to keep their hands off of her.

I met Goldie at the library's romance book club, and we bonded over our love of steamy romance novels and coffee drinks. She is with her men most of the time, but we still hang out a lot and talk on the phone nearly every day. She also has two-year-old triplets that I love to spoil. I'm their honorary auntie.

"*On my way!*" she texts back.

Ten minutes after I walk inside my house, Goldie is at the door. She gives me a tight hug. "Okay. Spill. What is going on that calls for ice cream?" She sets a few containers on the counter, and I grab two spoons.

"Have you ever heard of shifters?" I ask, taking a bite of my Haagen Daaz chocolate ice cream. So delicious!

Goldie suddenly looks uncomfortable. "Yes. Why do you ask?"

"Because I just met Granny's realtor, Damian Wolf, and he's a wolf shifter who says he's my fated mate and we are going to be together forever," I get out in one long breath.

"You are his mate? Oh my god! That is so great! I'm so happy for you!" She jumps up and down, then gives me another hug before pulling away. "Wait a sec. If you found each other, why are you here with me and not off with him?"

"I didn't even know shifters were real until about thirty minutes ago. I told him I needed a little space."

"Oh, honey. He's going to be busting down your door any second now. We'd better talk fast," she says while licking her spoonful of rocky road.

"So, you know about shifters?"

"Yep. That's fair to say."

"Do you know any?" I can tell by her silence that she does. "Who?"

"Well, we live in a town with a pretty big shifter population. There are tons of them. But the ones I know best are my husbands."

"What?!" I screech. "Oh my god! I can't believe you never told me!"

"I'm so sorry! They are really weird about it. The only people I've told are my parents, and now you."

"Are they wolves, too?"

"No. They are grizzly bears."

"Wow. Did it not freak you out to have that sprung on you?"

"Not at all. I had dreams about them for years before I found them, so I knew what I was getting into."

"So, when you are their fated mate, what's it like?"

"It is wonderful! They are obsessed with you. They don't want anyone else. They will do everything in their power to make you happy. And the sex? Oh. My. God. You will never want to get out of bed. They are also possessive as hell."

I have noticed that her husbands are crazy protective of her. They do seem to growl a lot, too. It all makes a lot of sense now that I think about it. "So you think that this is okay? I'm not crazy for jumping into a relationship with a man I just met?"

"Oh, honey. It would be crazy not to be with him if he's your mate. I'm telling you, it's the best thing in the world. It puts the romance novels we read to shame."

She puts the ice cream in my freezer for next time. "Now go get your wolf!" she says as she walks out the door.

"I will. Thank you." I give Goldie another hug, then go inside to freshen up. I send Damian a text to meet me here. I check my hair and makeup. My entire body hums with anticipation.

Twenty-Seven

Damian

I told Scarlett I would give her time, but my beast is already trying to break through and mark her. I won't be able to hold him back much longer. I got her address and am standing outside her cottage, pacing back and forth.

Goldie, the Bear brothers' wife, leaves and heads toward her car. They must be good friends if Scarlett invited her over. That bodes well since she is mated to three bear shifters. Maybe she can make Scarlett understand just how special finding your mate is. She turns and grins at me. "Bye, Wolf! Congratulations!" I smile and wave back at her.

I am doing everything I can to hold myself back when a text from Scarlett comes through on my phone, asking me to come over. I am ringing her doorbell seconds later.

"Damian! How on earth did you get here so fast?"

"I was already here. Waiting."

She smiles, sealing her fate. I push her inside with my body, slam the door, then push her up against it. "Have you learned a little more about shifters and mates, babe?" I ask, kissing her gently.

"Yes. I know a little more now," she says, closing her eyes. "I don't really understand all of this, but I don't want to stay away from you any longer. I ache for you."

"You have no idea how happy that makes me, sweetheart." She just gave me permission, and my beast is through waiting. I tear her dress open, making buttons fly in every direction. I rip her bra off, baring her succulent breasts. I squeeze her luscious tits, taking turns sucking on her sweet strawberry nipples until she climaxes.

"Damian!" She screams.

I caress every inch of her curvy body. Her skin feels like silk, and smells like vanilla and cinnamon. I take her mouth again, licking inside, and pulling her closer. "Where's your bedroom, sweetheart?"

"First door on the left." I pick her up and rush to her bedroom. I toss her on the bed, and rip her dress the rest of the way off, baring her gorgeous curves. Her perfect little pussy is bare and glistening with her juices.

"Mine," I growl, before devouring her sweetness with my mouth. Scarlett's scent is intoxicating, but her taste is even better. I will happily lick this sweet little cunt for the rest of my life. She screams again, gushing against my face. I tear off my shirt, then undo my slacks as quickly as possible. My big cock is already dripping pre-cum, ready to go.

She is lying on the bed, legs spread wide open, just waiting for me. Her large tits and tiny waist draw my attention. She has the perfect body. Perfect for fucking, and perfect for carrying and nursing my babies.

"So, I guess everything happens really fast with shifters and their mates?" she asks breathlessly, writhing on the bed.

"Yes, sweetheart. It does. You are my mate. I'm going to spend the next several days showing you that we are made for each other. I'm going to fuck you so good, you'll never want to get out of bed." She gushes again. Damn. She likes dirty talk. I am one lucky shifter.

Her eyes rake over me in appreciation. I can smell her arousal. It's driving me insane. I spend a little time loosening her up with my fingers and tongue. There's a lot of me to take, and I don't want to hurt my beautiful mate.

"Damn, baby. You are sopping wet for me." When I can't wait a second longer, I push the tip of my cock into her wet opening and enter heaven.

Twenty-Eight

Scarlett

Oh my god. I've never been so turned on. Damian is so sexy. I feel like I will die if I don't have him all the way inside me right this second. His giant cock is stretching me. I know pain is coming, but I don't care. I've never wanted anything so badly in all my life.

"Yes, Damian! More! Fuck me!"

"Fuck, Scarlett. You feel so good. Your sweet little pussy is squeezing the life out my cock, but you will take every inch of me. Once you do, I may never leave your hot little cunt."

With that, he pushes all the way in. It stings for a few seconds, but then I feel more pleasure than I could have ever imagined.

"I'm sorry, baby. I don't want to hurt you."

"I'm good now. Please don't stop."

"Never," he says. His eyes glow as he pounds into me harder and harder, making me lightheaded from orgasm after orgasm. "Mine!" he yells as he takes me, slamming the bed against the wall over and over again with the force of his thrusts. My neck starts tingling like crazy. He licks the exact place that tingles before biting me there. I feel pain for a moment, then even more pleasure as he explodes inside me, triggering one last orgasm from me, and sending me into a deep sleep.

A short time later, I feel Damian cleaning me with a damp washcloth. He is so sweet. I want to tell him that, but I can't keep my eyes open.

Twenty-Nine

Scarlett

I wake up feeling very confused. Why am in bed in the middle of the day? I roll over and land against Damian. Oh, right. That really wasn't a dream. I actually did have sex with a man I just met a few hours ago. A man who is apparently my fated mate.

I know this would sound crazy to anyone else, but as I take in Wolf's incredible body, I have no regrets. I know that I would absolutely, one hundred percent, do it all over again. He rolls onto his back, dislodging the covers. His beast of a cock is standing at attention, causing my mouth to water and moisture to pool between my legs.

I don't understand what is happening to me. Up until a short while ago, I had never had any interest whatsoever in having sex with anyone. I kind of thought I was asexual, but apparently not. I just had to find my mate to become a full fledged sex fiend. I am already starving for him again. Before I even realize what I'm doing, I move down his body and suck the tip of his cock into my mouth, making him moan. I am so hungry for him, I can't help myself.

"You taste so good," I say, swirling my tongue around his cock head like a lollipop.

"Damn, Scarlett. That feels so good, baby. Keep sucking that big cock," he says, pushing my mouth farther down on him. He soon loses control and starts fucking my mouth hard. I am having a tough time keeping up, but I love it. My eyes water, and my throat burns, but I love that Damian is so out of control. "Gonna come down your throat now." His dick hits the back of my throat and explodes. I greedily swallow every creamy drop. I barely touch my clit and come right along with him.

"Fuck, baby. That's a hell of a way to wake a man up," he says, trying to catch his breath.

"I don't seem to have any self control around you," I say, tracing patterns across his hairy chest.

"Believe me; the feeling is mutual."

Before I know it, I'm flat on my back again being fucked hard by my delicious man. He slams inside me repeatedly, causing the bed to creak hard, until it finally breaks.

"Oh, my god! I can't believe we broke the bed!" I giggle. It only takes me a second to forget all about it. Wolf throws the mattress on the floor like it weighs nothing, before tossing me on top of it and fucking me so hard I see stars.

Thirty

Damian

When I open my eyes, it's morning. I see my beautiful mate lying next to me. I stroke her cheek, then run my hands over her hips. Her porcelain skin shows scrapes and bruises from being taken so hard. That should bother me, but being the beast I am, I love seeing my marks on her. I know that she'll be feeling me whenever she walks; not only today, but always. I will never let her forget who she belongs to.

"Is it morning?" she asks, smiling up at me.

"It is, angel. I'd fix you some breakfast, but I'm a terrible cook."

"Good thing I'm a great cook," she says, jumping out of bed.

A short while later, my little red has laid out quite a spread for us-omelettes, pancakes, toast, and fruit. "This looks so good, sweetheart. Thank you. I'd say it is too much, but we both probably need some sustenance after yesterday."

She blushes adorably. "You are probably right. I am starving!"

We sit next to each other at her kitchen table. She tells me all about her job at the library, while I tell her about being a realtor. The conversation flows smoothly, never feeling forced or uncomfortable. We learn a lot about each other in a short time.

She's only wearing my shirt. She looks way better in it than I have ever thought about looking. When she finishes eating, she starts putting things in the dishwasher. When she bends over, I see that she has no panties on. I am on her in a flash.

"Oh! Damian!" she gasps as I bend her over and devour her sweet little cunt with my mouth. I put her on the kitchen island and lick her honey hole. It doesn't take long before she is begging for me.

"Please fuck me, Damian." I free my hungry cock and push inside, causing her to gasp.

"Are you too sore, baby?"

"No! Please don't stop."

"Not a chance," I say as I slam into her velvet heat faster and faster. It doesn't take long for her to come again. When her pussy pulses hard and squeezes my cock, it's all I can take. I let go, spilling stream after stream of cum inside my mate, and hoping that she is already pregnant.

Thirty-One

Scarlett

Later that day, we stop by Damian's to pick up some clothes for him. I look around as we walk inside. It's a nice place, but a little cold. No pictures, no paintings. The walls are completely bare.

"Sorry. I just moved in a short time ago, and haven't done any decorating. I didn't know I'd be bringing my mate home with me," he says nervously.

"It's fine," I reassure him with a quick kiss. Well, it was supposed to be a quick kiss. Before I know it, I have my clothes peeled off of me and am being flipped over on my hands and knees on his couch.

"It's been too long, sweetheart," he says as he massages my ass before slamming his cock in me from behind. "Yes!" we both cry out. "I'll never get enough of this sweet little pussy." Oh, god. His dirty talk really does it for me; just like everything else about him. "You are drenched, baby. You want my big cock fucking you?"

"Yes!" I scream. He slams into me again and again. My climax hits me suddenly. My pussy tightens around him hard, making him pour inside me. He pulls out, then picks me up like I weigh nothing.

"Little red, I think I need to give you a tour of my bedroom."

"Lead on, my big, bad, sexy wolf."

Thirty-Two

Damian

Some time later, we are lying in bed resting.

"Whose house?" I ask, thinking out loud.

"Whose house for what?"

"Whose house should we live in; mine or yours?"

"Whoa. We literally just met each other yesterday! Don't you think this is way too fast?"

"Baby, this is it. This is the real deal. You are it for me, and I am it for you. I have no doubts. There's no reason to wait. I want to move in together, wife you up, and put my baby in you as soon as possible."

"Oh, shit!" she says as it suddenly dawns on her. "We haven't used any protection!"

"No, we haven't. I will be thrilled if you are pregnant. I have been doing everything I can to knock you up."

She laughs. "You definitely have been filling me up every chance you get. I would love to have a baby with you, too. How about if we just live at my place for now and maybe build sometime down the road?"

"Works for me, sweetheart. Now, how soon can I get you to the altar?"

Thirty-Three

Scarlett

The answer is soon; very soon. I am getting ready for my wedding one week after meeting Damian Wolf. One week! It sounds insane, but it feels right. When you know, you know. If you are not with a shifter, it's just a little tough to understand. And if you are, lucky you!

Goldie and Granny zip up my dress. As I look at my reflection in the mirror, I've never felt so beautiful. I look like a princess with my gorgeous white gown that glitters with my every move. I glow with happiness, and it's all because of my handsome fiance.

A short while later, I am walking down the aisle to a very sexy, and very impatient, Damian. "It's about time. I was about to come find you," he says, kissing my cheek. "You look stunning."

"Thank you, baby. You look very handsome." All dressed in a tux, he looks scrumptious. His biceps are testing the strength of his sleeves. He looks like he might hulk out and bust through at any time. As he takes my hand, I realize I have no doubts whatsoever that this is who I want to spend my life with. It doesn't matter how quickly it happened. I know that he is my person.

After a speedy ceremony, the minister pronounces us husband and wife, and Damian lays a borderline x-rated kiss on me. He holds the back of my neck while his mouth takes mine over and over again until I can't think straight. We are wrapped in each others arms, oblivious to everything else. Finally, the minister clearing his throat breaks through my haze of lust. My face gets a little red, but I don't care too much. I wouldn't change anything about my sexy husband, including his very public claiming of me.

"To be continued," he whispers in my ear.

"I can't wait."

Thirty-Four

Damian

For a small reception, there are a lot of people here. Apparently, most of our small town came out for the wedding. It's great that people are so friendly here; don't get me wrong. The problem is I need inside my wife. Now. She insisted that we spend the night before our wedding apart. I was not too happy about it. It's the first night I've slept alone since finding her, and it will be the last one if I have anything to say about it.

Scarlett is across the room talking to some people I don't recognize. I stalk over to her and take her hand. "Baby, can you help me with something really quick?"

"Sure," she smiles up at me.

I'm practically dragging her to a small room in the back of the chapel. "Where are we going?"

I shut us in, and push her against the door. "I need your sweet pussy right now." I push up the poofy dress to get to her.

"Yesss," she hisses as I push her panties to the side and sink my fingers inside her wetness. "Damian!" she screams, gushing on my fingers. I lick them clean.

"So fucking delicious." She licks her lips as I undo my pants. My cock springs out, slapping against my stomach. I'm already dripping pre-cum. I can't get inside my bride quick enough. "Come lie down on the couch. Hold your dress up and spread your legs. Let us have a quick preview of our honeymoon."

She does what I tell her. Within seconds, I am pumping in and out of her sweet pussy. I know that neither of us are going to last long. When she screams again, her sweet little cunt milks every drop of cum out of me. We lie there for a few minutes, catching our breath.

"Come on, sweetheart," I say, pulling her up. We straighten her dress out the best we can, and try not to look like we just ducked out of our reception to have sex. Considering how many shifters are here, they probably already know. I give her another kiss to tide us over. "Let's get this reception over with so we can start our honeymoon."

Thirty-Five

Scarlett

The reception went on longer than either of us would have liked, but it was pretty awesome to have all of our friends and family in one place. We are finally back at my house. We are leaving for our honeymoon in Bora Bora tomorrow.

"Come here, little red," Damian says in his sexy voice.

"Me? What could the big, bad, sexy wolf possibly want with little old me?" I say, helping my new husband out of his dress clothes.

"Everything."

"Oh, my, Mr. Wolf. What big, strong arms you have."

"The better to hold you with, my dear."

"What big hands you have."

"The better to touch you with, my dear."

"What big teeth you have."

"The better to eat you with, my dear." He grins, stripping his underwear off. His cock is at full attention; dripping and ready for me.

"Oh, Mr. Wolf, what a big, hard cock you have!" I say, stroking him, and licking his pre-cum from my fingers.

"The better to fuck you with, my dear," he says, tossing me down on the bed. I giggle, then help him take my dress off before he destroys it like he has way too many of my clothes already.

"There's a zipper on the side."

"Good thing. This dress was about to be ripped off your sexy little body." He unzips my dress and sets it on an armchair before returning to me. "Now, little red, you are all mine. You look sexy as fuck in this outfit."

I smile as he kisses and teases his way down my sexy bridal lingerie, complete with garters and stockings. He kisses my mouth before working his way down my neck and chest, eliciting appreciative moans from me. He drags my teddy down, cupping my breasts and sucking them. I arch off the bed with the pleasure of it. He tosses the garment over his shoulder. I move to take off my thigh high stockings.

"Leave them on while I fuck you. They are sexy as hell, baby."

"As you wish." His mouth zeroes in on my pussy, devouring me whole. "Oh, my god!" His tongue laps at me, drinking down my orgasms and setting me off again. He bites down on my clit and I come hard, screaming his name.

While I'm catching my breath, he climbs on top of me. "I'm nowhere near done with you, sweetheart," he says as he thrusts his throbbing cock inside me, causing me to gush again. "I'll never get enough of you, Scarlett. You are mine. Now and always."

"And you are mine," I say, coming again. "Fuck me harder, baby."

"Your wish is my command," he says, thrusting even harder. I feel his body tense before he gushes inside of me, sending me into another orgasm.

"I love you so much, Mrs. Wolf."

"I love you, too, Mr. Wolf."

Thirty-Six

Epilogue 1-Scarlett

One year later...

What a difference a year makes. I have gone from being single and alone to being happily married with a gorgeous husband and our beautiful baby girl, Piper. Damian managed to get me pregnant right off the bat. She's an absolute angel, and looks like my mini me.

"Where are my beautiful girls?" My husband calls out, as he walks in the front door.

"Right here!" I call from the living room. He comes in and kisses Piper, then me.

"I've missed you, sweetheart."

I laugh. "It's only been two hours since you left."

"I know, but even that is too long."

"I missed you, too."

"Are you two up to going for a ride? There's something I want to show you."

A few minutes later, we load up in our roomy SUV, headed to a surprise destination. We soon pull up in front of a gorgeous home. "Where are we?"

"I want you to keep an open mind. I just got the listing for this house. I know we talked about building, but I think you will love this place."

He unhooks Piper's baby seat, swinging it slowly around, trying to keep her asleep for the time being. When we walk inside, I am stunned. If you had asked me to describe my dream house, this would be it. Soaring ceilings, a massive fireplace, wood beams, and a kitchen that Gordon Ramsey would be jealous of. "Wow! It's gorgeous!"

There is a huge backyard, and even a game room. He takes me through the rest of the house. There are five bedrooms, which we apparently need since Wolf is determined to keep me knocked up. I just had Piper a few months ago, but I'm already pregnant again, thanks to my ravenous husband and his super sperm.

"Well, what do you think?"

"I love it!"

"I'm so glad. I could picture us here as soon as I saw it. I'll put in an offer today. But first, I think we need to christen our new house."

"Ooh, I like the way you think."

Thirty-Seven

Epilogue 2-Damian

Ten years later...

It's quiet in the house when I walk in, which is very unusual. With six kids, quiet just doesn't happen very often; or ever. A movement outside catches my eye. I walk out the back door and am greeted with chaos. This is more like it. Laughing, screaming, running. And wolves. Lots of wolves.

"There you are! Please deal with this. Your children are out of control." Scarlett says, while kissing me softly. When they are angels, they are hers. When they are a mess, they are mine. Our two youngest just started shifting last week. Now that all six of them can shift, they race around every chance they get, destroying everything in their path. Our patio furniture is strewn about and shredded. It looks like our backyard got hit by a tornado.

"Give me an hour, baby. I'll wear them out." I strip and change into my wolf form. I spend the next hour racing with the kids in the woods behind our house until they are finally beat. "Go take baths and get ready for bed." The kids all go inside, wrapping themselves in beach towels. A short while later, everyone is down for the count.

"Now it's time for this wolf to play with little red," I say as I close our bedroom door. Scarlett is under the covers, smiling mischievously at me.

"What could you possible want with me, Mr. Wolf?" she bats her eyelashes at me. She tosses the covers aside, revealing her gorgeous, naked body.

"Everything. I want everything with you," I growl, tossing my clothes aside and pinning my wife down in one quick move.

"You can have whatever you want from me," she says, thrusting her hips against my hardness. I'm already leaking pre-cum. Even after all these years, my wife turns me on without even trying. Within seconds, I'm inside her; my favorite place to be. I'm so lucky to have found my mate.

"Fuck, Scarlett. You feel too good. I'll never last."

"Then don't. Come inside me. Give me another baby."

That's all it takes. She knows that nothing makes me lose control like the idea of knocking her up. I pound into her until I feel her pussy pulsing and clenching hard around my cock. I let go, filling her with enough cum to make her pregnant twenty times over.

I curl her up against me. "I love you so much, Scarlett."

"I love you, too, Damian. I'm so glad I found my big, bad, sexy wolf."

He laughs. "And I'm so glad I found my beautiful, perfect, little red."

Little red and her wolf lived happily ever after.

THE END

Thirty-Eight

Chapter 38

Once Upon A Time:
Twisted Sexy
Fairy Tales
ENTICING
Ella
LACY JANE

Thirty-Nine

Ella

"You have got to be kidding me," I mumble to myself as Katherine, my evil stepmother, yells at me to come downstairs to entertain her son, Ken, who she insists is my future husband. Unfortunately, my extremely slimy stepbrother holds no appeal for me. Why she thinks we would be perfect together, I have no clue.

"Ella!" she screeches.

"Jeez. Coming."

I throw on a pair of sweats, and don't bother fixing my hair or makeup. I'm sure I look terrible; at least I hope so. When Ken looks at me like he'd like to feast on me, it seriously makes me want to vomit.

So, yeah. This is my life. My mom passed away when I was still a baby, and my dad died of a heart attack three years ago, shortly after getting married to Katherine. I was completely devastated. Not only did I lose my dad, but I was left with a stepmom and stepbrother who I can't stand. Some of my friends call me Cinderella as a joke. So fucking funny, right? I don't have stepsisters, but I do have the evil stepmother and a stepbrother who gives me the absolute heebie-jeebies.

The only reason they stay here is that we live in a freaking castle (I'm not even kidding) and their every want and need is taken care of. They stay out of my way most of the time, and I stay out of theirs. That is what my life has been like for the last few years. I wish they would just leave, but that's not happening anytime soon. Apparently, my father put a clause in his will that they could live here indefinitely. Yikes.

I walk downstairs, feeling like I'm on my way to the gallows. Ken looks at me like I'm a steak dinner. He licks his lips, and pushes back his greasy black hair, trying to cover the bald spots. I'm really not superficial, but this man just grosses me out in every way. From the way he looks, to his god awful smell, to his clammy hands that try to wander. Yuck. Just yuck.

He takes a step toward me, causing my dog to bark ferociously at him. "Good dog, Cujo," I say under my breath. I pick up my beloved chihuahua mix and hold him close. He is always by my side. He is very aptly named. He loves me, tolerates a select few, and actively despises Ken and Katherine. I think he happens to be a fabulous judge of character.

"That fucking dog is a menace. When we get married, he will have to go."

"Oh my god! We are not getting married! Not now! Not ever! And do not threaten my dog!" I cuddle Cujo, snuggling his soft black and white fur, and walk outside with him. Maybe I just need to move out. I know that I have money, but I don't come into most of it until I am twenty-five or married. Unfortunately, I have no romantic prospects besides Ken. Gross. I would rather be destitute. For now, any expenses go through Katherine to be approved before being sent to the executor of Dad's trust. Let me tell you, she's pretty fucking stingy; unless it comes to something for her.

Don't get me wrong; I really can't complain. I live in a huge castle, I have a car, a phone, a clothing allowance, etc. I'm not poor by any means, but there's nothing worse than having to ask Katherine if I can have money for something. My father set it up where I would get a bit of money put in my account each month, so I mostly get by on that.

School has always been easy for me. I graduated from high school a couple of years early, then took college courses online and just finished a masters in business. I just need to decide what to do with it. Not bad for having just turned twenty-one a few days ago. Maybe now is the time to start thinking about getting the hell out of dodge and starting a life somewhere far away from Katherine and Ken.

Once Cujo finishes up outside, the two of us walk back upstairs to my room. I lock the door and throw myself on my plush bed. This is the only home I've ever known, but it really hasn't felt like it since Dad died. "What should we do, Cujo? Where should we go? Don't worry, wherever I go, you go." His ears perk up, and he gives me sweet doggy kisses.

My dad let me pick him out at the animal shelter five years ago for my sixteenth birthday. He had wanted to get me an expensive, purebred dog, but I explained that I wanted to rescue an unwanted dog from the local animal shelter. When we went there, they told us that Cujo was about to be euthanized because he was too mean. I went over to him (against their advice) and picked him up. He gave me doggy kisses all over my face. It was love at first sight for both of us. We've been inseparable ever since.

My phone rings with my bestie's ringtone. I smile, looking at the goofy picture of the two of us that pops up whenever she calls. "Hey, Shelly. What's up?"

"You are not going to believe this. The Sterling family is having a full on ball at their estate this Saturday, and we are going!"

I laugh. "Why on earth would we go to a ball?"

"Do you remember me telling you about Jeremy Strong?"

I roll my eyes. "Hmmm. Let me think…oh, yeah. The man that you've been obsessed with since you first saw him when you interviewed at Sterling Enterprises last month? That guy? Now that he's your boss, you probably only mention him twenty or thirty times a day."

"Okay. So, I might be crushing on him just a teeny bit. Anyway, he is going, and he wants me to go with him! I know it's a work thing, but maybe I can finally get his attention and it can be more. I had him put you on the guest list, too. We will have to have a girl's day on Saturday to get ready for it; hair, nails, ball gowns. I'm picking you up first thing Saturday morning!"

Shelly is a force of nature. It's easier to just give in than to try and fight her on something when she has her mind made up. I laugh. "Okay. It sounds like I don't have a choice."

"Nope. You don't. I'll see you bright and early Saturday. We can drop Cujo off with Mom, then spend the day getting beautiful."

I hang up the phone and turn to Cujo. "Well, it looks like Cinderella is going to the ball."

Forty

Prince

A fucking ball. My mother is putting on a ball as a way to throw every available female at me at once in hopes of getting grandchildren ASAP. I really don't have time to deal with this shit.

I work way too much as it is, trying to prove myself to my parents. Let me tell you, it's a losing battle. I have worked for my family's company, Sterling Enterprises, for most of my life. That's not an exaggeration. I started working part time there when I was barely old enough to read and write. Before that, I would sit in my father's office while he explained the importance of my legacy to me.

Sterling Enterprises was founded by my great-great-great grandfather. It has been passed down to each generation, with each of them acquiring even more wealth. As an only child, I have been told my entire life that I would run the company one day. The problem is, now that the time is finally here, my dad doesn't want to give up control.

Since graduating from Harvard Business School fifteen years ago, I have been the company's chief financial officer. I have been gradually trying to bring us into the twenty-first century, but I'm dealing with a bunch of dinosaurs. Most of the board members are older than my father, and just don't understand what all the fuss is about this thing called the internet. I really wish I was joking. It nearly took an act of congress for them to agree to let us set up a company website.

Anyhow, my mother has decided that I should be married; the sooner the better. That's why she will be inviting every socialite in the greater tri-state area to this ball. Don't get me wrong; I am not opposed to marriage. I just haven't found anyone that makes my heart sing. Yes, I realize how corny that sounds. I've always assumed that when I met my soulmate, it would be love at first sight. Maybe I've watched too many Hallmark movies with my mother.

I'm not single due to lack of interest. Not to brag, but I'm considered a catch. I hit the gym most days, and I'm told I am classically handsome, whatever the hell that means. I was chosen as New York City's most eligible bachelor this year; A dubious distinction, I assure you. The problem is the women who want to be Mrs. Prince Sterling only want me because of the lifestyle I can give them. All they see are dollar signs. They are fucking mercenary.

Little did I know, my dream girl was about to fall right into my arms.

Forty-One

Ella

Shelly tells me stories that are making me laugh so hard, my sides hurt. That's the way it always is with her. She is my favorite person in the world. She cracks me up again, making me snort laugh, which just sets her off laughing harder.

We have been best friends since kindergarten. She walked up to me, introduced herself, and told me we were now besties. We've been together ever since.

The manicurists glare at us. They don't seem to be very fun. I mean, jeez. Lighten up already. We are finishing up our manicures and pedicures. After that, we are finding dresses, then getting our hair and makeup done. Shelly is determined to get Jeremy's attention. Personally, I'm just glad to get out of the house for the night. Shelly's mom is watching Cujo since I don't trust Katherine with him at all, and he does kind of hate her.

By early afternoon, I am beat. Shelly has dragged me to three stores so far, looking for the perfect dress. Neither of us has found any we like. When we walk in to *Your Fairy Godmother's*, I think we may have finally hit pay dirt.

There are dresses as far as the eye can see, and every one of them is absolutely stunning.

"Oh my gosh, El! This is it!" Shelly touches an exquisite dress that shimmers as it moves. She scrambles to the dressing room. "Wow! It's perfect!" she exclaims.

"Well, let's see it." Shelly walks out, looking the best I've ever seen her look. "Wow! You look gorgeous!" The bodice hugs her curves, and the color accentuates her beauty. "Jeremy won't know what hit him."

"From your lips to God's ears."

Since she found the perfect dress, I am a little more optimistic about finding one for myself. I finally find it. It is a beautiful pale blue color, but there is something magical about it. The lights dance across it, making it change colors as it moves. When I try it on, it fits like a glove. I have never felt more beautiful. Shelly finds a tiara and puts it on top of my head.

"Perfect! You look every inch a princess!" enthuses an adorable little old lady. "I'm Nan, the owner. You can just call me your fairy godmother. Your prince won't know what hit him."

I laugh. "I don't have a prince, but thank you." Soon after, we get our hair and makeup done, then drive to Shelly's to get dressed, having no idea that both of our lives are about to drastically change.

Forty-Two

Ella

When Shelly opens the door to Jeremy, he looks stunned. She has been telling me that he has no interest in her whatsoever. Boy, did she ever get that wrong! I can tell by the way he devours her with his eyes that he is totally besotted.

"Damn, you look beautiful, Shelly," he says in a hoarse voice.

"Thank you. You look very handsome."

He escorts us to a limo, never taking his hand off of Shelly's back. Once we get inside, it is even worse. I definitely feel like a third wheel. I'm not sure they even notice I'm here. All they are doing is staring at each other, but they are basically eye fucking each other at this point. His hand keeps caressing further and further up her leg. Good grief. Hopefully, they can behave themselves until we get to the ball. Get a room!

Before things get out of hand, we pull up in front of a stately mansion. "Whoa. This place is huge!" We are escorted through security, then line up to be announced. We are going to be walking down a really long staircase in front of a ton of people. I'm really regretting wearing sky high heels right now.

Forty-Three

Prince

If another socialite asks me how rich I am, I may resort to homicide. Do they really think I'm going to be impressed with someone who obviously only wants my money? Every woman I've met so far is vapid, shallow, and has no possibility of ever becoming my wife.

I look up to see my friend, Jeremy, arriving with his assistant, Shelly. He confessed to me recently how smitten he is with her. He looks like he's ready to claim her in front of everyone. Good for him. She looks like she's into him, too. I hope it works out for them. He's a good friend who deserves happiness.

"Miss Ella James," Jameson, our butler, announces. I look up with no interest whatsoever until I see her. Time stands still. She looks like a fairy tale princess. Beautiful blonde hair piled in an updo, curves that would make a centerfold envious, and puffy little pink lips that were made to drive men insane. Her sparkly blue dress changes colors as she moves, hypnotizing me. My body is on high alert, and my cock is rock fucking hard. There is no doubt in my mind that this beauty is my future wife.

She walks down the stairs toward me, commanding all of my attention. When she gets toward the bottom, she trips over her long dress, and starts to fall. I spring into action and catch her just in time. I hold her against me, staring into her stunned gray eyes.

"I had no idea that the woman of my dreams would literally fall right into my arms. Hello, beautiful. I'm Prince Sterling."

"I..I'm Ella. It's very nice to meet you. Thank you for catching me."

"You are very welcome, Ella." She feels perfect in my arms. I plan to never let her go.

My mother walks over to me, rattling on about all of the debutantes I need to meet. I don't even let her finish. "Don't bother, Mother. The search is over. I'm marrying Ella."

Forty-Four

Ella

His mother lets out a gasp, but then has a huge smile on her face. "Oh, Prince. I am so happy for you," she says, patting his back. "Welcome to the family, dear!"

Say what now? This absolutely gorgeous man, Prince Sterling, is holding me against his body, short circuiting my brain. Did he just tell his mother we were getting married? I obviously heard him wrong or he just has a really weird sense of humor.

I was so nervous walking down the stairs in these high heels that I didn't even see him until he caught me, saving me from a hard fall and terrible embarrassment. Shelly had said that tons of women were dying to be Mrs. Prince Sterling. I thought that must have been an exaggeration, but now that I've seen him up close and personal, I think she might have been understating it.

Who wouldn't want to be married to this sexy beast? He has got to be the hottest man I have ever laid eyes on. At well over six feet tall, he dwarfs my five feet three inches, even in heels. Not only is he tall; he's huge *everywhere*.

He looks like he lives in the gym or chops wood every day. His arms are muscled up, as is his chest, which I realize I'm still touching. Even if he was dirt poor, there would still be tons of women falling at his feet.

I go to pull away, but he tugs me closer. "Let's dance."

"Of course." He holds me in his arms, and time seems to stand still. It's like something out of a fairy tale. He spins me around the dance floor while asking me questions about myself and answering mine about him. I hope he doesn't notice the goosebumps all over my body. Thankfully, he can't see the butterflies in my stomach that he is causing.

We hear a commotion and turn to see Jeremy throwing Shelly over his shoulder. "Mine!" he yells as he spanks her butt and walks out the door with her pounding her fists against his back.

"Um, is your friend okay?"

I laugh. "Yes. She's been trying to get Jeremy's attention for the last month. I think it's safe to say she has it now."

"He's a good man, and I know for a fact that he's crazy about your friend."

"I'm glad to hear it. She's the best."

I go on to tell him all about Cujo, Shelly, Dad, Katherine, and Ken. He growls a lot when I mention him. He tells me a lot about his family and his company. The entire time, he holds me close, nuzzling the side of my neck, and stroking my back. His lips gently touch my ear and neck, making my nipples push uncomfortably against my bra and completely soaking my panties. This incredibly hot man is driving me crazy with desire.

After some time has passed, he pulls me even closer, rubbing his extremely hard cock against me. The sheer size of it causes me to gasp. I can't believe this sexy man is so turned on by me.

"Come, my love. Let's go somewhere quiet to talk." I look up into his hypnotic chocolate eyes and nod. His face is so handsome, with his close trimmed beard and strong jaw. His jet black hair is a little on the long side, like it needs a cut, but it suits him perfectly.

He pulls me down the hall. I have no idea where we are going, but I can't wait to find out. I realize that I would follow this man anywhere.

Forty-Five

Prince

I hadn't been very optimistic about finding a wife tonight, but I am thrilled to have been sorely mistaken. Ella is stunning. I practically drag her from the ball to my living quarters. She giggles, which is fucking adorable.

I assumed that when I met my soulmate, I would feel warm and fuzzy toward her. I had no idea that I would feel such overwhelming desire that I would barely be able to restrain from throwing her down and claiming her in front of everyone. The last hour spent dancing with her in my arms was wonderful, but also pure torture. My cock has never been so hard.

I lock the door behind us and turn to my beautiful bride-to-be. "Now, where were we?"

"You said we needed to talk," she says, nervously licking her lips.

"We do need to talk, but first I need to do this," I say, before claiming her soft lips in a kiss. She moans, opening her mouth. I slide my tongue inside, taking my time. Damn, she tastes good. Chocolate and vanilla mixed with a taste that only belongs to her, and I am already addicted to it. When I let her up for air, she touches her puffy lips, looking stunned.

"Damn, princess, feel what you do to me." I push her hand against my hard cock, making her gasp. Her eyes dilate as she pulls me back against her. This time it's her that takes my mouth with a hunger that matches mine. I pull her harder against me, rubbing against her sweet pussy as best as I can with her dress cockblocking me.

"If you want to stop, you need to tell me now. I'm hanging on by a thread, Ella."

"We really shouldn't do this. We don't even know each other, but I don't want to stop" she says, while rubbing her legs against each other and kissing me hungrily. Damn, she is so sexy. She wants me just as much as I want her.

"We have the rest of our lives to get to know each other, but right now, I really need to fuck your sweet little pussy."

I tear the dress from her, devouring her with my eyes. "Jesus. You are stunning," I say, admiring her curves clad in only a lace bra and panties.

Forty-Six

Ella

Oh, lord. With any other man, I would find his crude talk disgusting. With Prince, though, I find it ridiculously hot. My pussy has never been this wet before. I never really felt any kind of sexual desire before meeting him. Now, I'm consumed with it.

I am standing nearly naked in front of a man I met a little over an hour ago. This is way too quick, right? I don't know what is wrong with me. I should feel ashamed, but instead I just feel turned on.

I feel a burst of confidence as I see the large bulge straining at the front of his pants. I grip his hardness through his clothes, causing him to moan. "If you plan to fuck me, you have way too many clothes on." His eyes darken with desire, and he hurriedly strips his tux off.

Damn, but this man is hot. I thought he looked incredibly handsome with his tuxedo on, but as he reveals his chiseled body to me, I have to say he looks even better without it. His chest is muscular and hairy. I can't wait to feel it against me, along with the rest of him.

He tugs down his boxers, revealing a huge, hard cock. I lick my lips as I take him all in. His cock head is purple and angry looking, and already leaking precum. Veins run down his cock to his heavy balls. The ache inside me intensifies, making more wetness leak down my legs. I know that this man alone can make it all better.

He stalks toward me, squeezing his cock and breathing heavily. He rips my bra and panties from me in no time at all, and pushes me down on the bed. "Spread your legs, sweetheart. Show me that sweet pussy."

Forty-Seven

Prince

It is taking every ounce of my control not to blow like a teenage boy. Ella is perfect. So beautiful. So sweet. So mine. "Fuck, baby. You are gorgeous." I kiss her lips softly, then kiss her neck, eliciting moans from her .

I caress her breasts, pinching each nipple before sucking on each in turn. "Yessss!" she hisses. I squeeze harder, then kiss my way down her soft stomach and press my mouth to each hip before heading toward the promise land.

Her sweet little pussy is so pretty and pink. It is bare and dripping with her arousal. I take a deep breath and my mouth waters. I can't deny either of us any longer. I lick her sweet, spicy little cunt. "You are so fucking delicious. Gonna eat your sweetness every day."

"Oh my god! Prince, it feels so good!" she yells as I shove my tongue in her tiny hole, kissing and sucking for all I'm worth. She tugs my hair, pushing me even harder into her sweet pussy as she arches off the bed. I tease her for a few minutes before sucking her clit into my mouth, making her shatter.

She screams my name as she comes, gushing all over my face. I greedily lick up every drop. "Wow," she says shakily.

"Oh, sweetheart. You ain't seen nothing yet." I push her flat with my body, and thrust the head of my cock into her sweet heat, causing us both to moan.

"More," she cries, digging her fingernails into my back. I thrust in a little bit at a time.

"Fuck, you are so tight. You feel so good, baby. I'll fuck you so hard, you won't be able to walk without feeling me. Gonna make you mine." The wetness I feel tells me she likes my words. I slide further in until I feel a thin barrier. I can't believe my sweet angel has never been touched. I will be her first and only. "You kept this sweet little pussy all for me, didn't you, princess?"

"Yes!" she yells.

"Mine!" I scream as I punch through and bottom out. "Fuck!!!" I yell as I come deep inside her. Her wet heat feels so good; I couldn't stop myself. The good news is I'm still hard as a fucking rock. "Are you okay, princess?" I ask, gently stroking her face.

"Yes. Please don't stop."

"Not a fucking chance."

Forty-Eight

Ella

I feel so full. Prince's enormous cock has me so stretched out, but I've never felt anything better. At least until he starts thrusting. "Oh, fuck!" I scream. "Yes!!!"

"Gonna come inside you again and again, sweetheart. Gonna put my baby in you."

"Oh, god." He can't possibly mean that, but I hope he does. The idea turns me on even more. Soon he is thrusting so hard, the bed is slamming against the wall.

"Come for me, princess." I do as he commands, gushing all over his huge cock, just as I feel him come deep inside me. I had no idea a man could release so much cum. I feel the warmth dripping down my thighs. I try to catch my breath.

He pulls me against him, kissing me deeply. "I don't want to scare you, baby, but I love you."

I feel my eyes leaking tears as my heart fills with joy. "I love you, too, Prince."

"Marry me."

Forty-Nine

Prince

"You are crazy, but yes. I will marry you."

"Thank God. I really didn't want to tie you to the bed until I convinced you, but I would have."

She smiles. "On second thought, maybe I should have said no."

"No take backs, baby. You are mine."

"Well…I am, but why don't you show me what you would have done to convince me."

"Absolutely. Down on your knees. Get ready to take your punishment." She smiles as she lowers herself in front of me. I sit on the bed so that she can reach me.

"I've never done this before. Show me what you like." My cock stands at attention again, ready to pump into her hot little mouth. She licks the head, making me spurt a little bit of cum already. She strokes me as she sucks. Then she licks me like a lollipop. "Mmmm," she hums, licking the cream leaking out of the tip. "So good." She then deep throats me in one quick motion.

"Fuck, sweetheart. I'm gonna come again." She amps up her efforts, hollowing her cheeks and sucking me for all she's worth. As I come inside the wet heat of her mouth, she rubs her little clit, coming along with me.

"I'm not done with you yet, princess." I toss her onto the bed, licking the sweetness between her legs until she comes again, screaming my name. I slam my cock all the way inside her heat. This time I don't go easy on her. I fuck her hard, like we both want.

"Yes! Oh my god! You feel so good!"

"You do, too, baby. Your tight little pussy is gonna milk all the cum from my body." A few more thrusts, and we both come once more. I pull her against me, kissing her until we both fall asleep wrapped in each others arms.

Fifty

Ella

I wake up, feeling sore in places I've never been sore before. My pussy has been well used, but it already wants more. I feel so warm and protected. I move and find myself pinned under a very hard male body. Mmmm. What a way to start the day.

"Good morning, my princess."

"Good morning."

He kisses me tenderly before trailing kisses down my body. My body remembers him. I am already on fire again. I'm unable to stop my hips from thrusting toward him, seeking the pleasure that only he can give me.

"Let me taste you again, baby. Then I will fuck you until you are overflowing with my cum."

I feel wetness pooling between my legs again. I would never have thought dirty talk would do it for me, but with him, it definitely does. Of course, everything he does turns me on, so I shouldn't be so surprised.

Soon, he is devouring my pussy like he's starving for it. He flicks my clit, making me scream out his name as I orgasm again. Before I have a chance to recover, he is slamming inside me. All thoughts leave my head. All I can do is feel. His hard cock fucking me feels so good. Before I know it, I orgasm so hard, I nearly pass out.

"Gonna get you pregnant, princess," he says as he explodes inside me, sending me into yet another release. I hope he means everything he says, because I am already head over heels in love with Prince Sterling.

Fifty-One

Prince

Damn. I really wish I didn't have to go out of town on business so soon after finding my bride. Unfortunately, this is an extremely important meeting that I can't miss. I kiss Ella once more, missing her already.

"It's okay, Prince. I have to go get Cujo from Shelly's mom and take care of some things at home anyway."

"I don't want you to leave. Why don't you just stay here while I'm gone? You can bring Cujo, too."

She laughs. "Once you meet him, you might want to retract your offer."

"Not a chance. No take backs. Remember? You are mine. I love you. I will love your dog, too."

I give her a long, leisurely kiss before making myself step away. "Here is a key. The staff will get you anything you like. I'll be back tomorrow night."

"Okay. Have a safe trip. I love you."

"I love you, too, baby. More than you'll ever know."

I turn away, feeling like I'm leaving half of my heart behind. I have a bad feeling about this, but I'm sure it's all in my head.

Fifty-Two

Ella

I pick up Cujo from Shelly's mom. He is happy to see me, but he's pouting and making it known that he is not thrilled about having been left overnight. "Don't worry, Cujo. We'll get you a pup cup from 7Brew." He wags his tail and gives me a kiss. All is forgiven.

At 7Brew, he barks and snaps at the workers. "I'm so sorry. He doesn't like anyone much but me." They laugh, seeming unfazed by his rude behavior. It makes me feel bad, though. "Why do you have to be such a meanie?" He devours his pup cup, then smirks at me. He's a little shit, but I love him to death.

I head to my house, thinking about the future for the first time in a positive way. I am leaving and getting away from my evil stepmom and her creepy as shit son. I can't wait!

I grab Cujo and head inside, only to be met in the foyer by Katherine. "Where the hell have you been?" she screeches.

"At a ball. Calm down." I know she wasn't worried about me in the slightest. I have no idea why she is having such a conniption. She has never cared where I went before.

"I heard that you were with Prince Sterling and he said he was going to marry you." I smile. Did everyone hear him say that?

"I suppose so. I'll be moving out as soon as possible. I'm sure you two will enjoy having more space."

"Yeah. That won't be happening. You won't be marrying him. Ken!" she yells.

"Whatever. As soon as I pack a bag, I am out of here." I turn to go to my room, but am stopped by creepy Ken.

"Sorry, but you aren't going anywhere." He raises his hand and everything goes black.

Fifty-Three

Ella

Damn, my head hurts. I wake to Cujo whimpering and kissing my face. "I'm okay, baby." As I say that, though, I'm not so sure. Where the heck am I? I look around the room. It has one tiny window up high. Too small for me to get through, and I don't see any way to get high enough up to get Cujo through it. Even if I did, what could he do? Go to the police and bark?

I try the door, finding that it is locked. What the fuck is going on? I was on cloud nine about moving in with Prince when creepy Ken knocked me out and apparently dragged me to this room. It looks like a fucking dungeon. Our house is an old castle with lots of rooms, but I seriously didn't know we had a dungeon. And why am I here? Why do they care if I leave? I don't understand, but I do know I have to get out of here as soon as possible.

Unfortunately, Prince won't be back until tomorrow night and Shelly wasn't at home today, so it will probably be late tomorrow before anyone realizes I'm missing. I snuggle with Cujo and pray that we remain unharmed until then.

Fifty-Four

Prince

I sit through a series of important meetings without absorbing anything. My instincts are screaming at me to get back to Ella. Maybe it's just because our relationship is so new. We take a break and I put in a call to her. It goes straight to voicemail. I try again and it does the same. I call the house, only to find that she hasn't shown up yet. She should have been there hours ago.

The niggling worry in my gut increases tenfold, and I race out of the meeting. "So sorry. Family emergency. I have to go." I don't wait for my secretary or anyone else. I race down to my car and direct the driver back to the airport. I am hopping on my jet and getting back to my princess as soon as possible.

Once I'm in the air, I call Jeremy. I know he can put me in touch with his assistant, who is Ella's best friend. "Hey, Jeremy. Sorry to bother you, but I need to know how to reach your assistant." He growls through the phone at me. What the fuck?

"Why do you need to get a hold of her?" he asks in a possessive tone I've never heard from him before.

"Because I'm marrying Ella and she has disappeared."

"What?" I hear her friend screech. "Give me the phone, you neanderthal. You're marrying her? What do you mean she has disappeared?"

"I had to go out of town for a meeting. She was supposed to go get Cujo, then pack some stuff and go back to my house. She never showed and she's not answering my calls or messages."

"That's really not like her. I bet that bitch of a stepmom has done something to her. I'll go over there right now!"

"The hell you will, sweetheart," Jeremy says in a tone that brooks no argument.

"She's my best friend!"

"And you are my woman. Where you go, I go."

"Okay, fine."

"I touch down in fifteen minutes. Meet me at the airport and we'll all go together."

I spend the next few minutes talking with the police chief about the situation. Ella hasn't been gone long enough to file a missing persons report, but he does promise to see what dirt he can dig up on the stepmom. I hang up the phone, anxiety clawing at my throat.

"Hang on, princess. I'm coming to rescue you."

Fifty-Five

Ella

I wish I knew how long we've been down here. It seems like forever. They took my apple watch and iPhone, so I really have no idea. I do know that I'm starving, so it's definitely been awhile.

Cujo and I nod off for a bit. We sleep pretty soundly, considering we are sleeping on a cold stone floor. When I wake up, Cujo is barking his head off. It's then that I realize a car is pulling up outside. "Help!!!" I scream repeatedly at the top of my lungs. I hope whoever it is can hear us.

Fifty-Six

Prince

We pull up in front of Ella's house; well, castle. My mother will be thrilled to know that Ella isn't after my money. She appears to have plenty of her own. The three of us pound on the door and are greeted by an older woman with hard features.

"The evil stepmom, I presume?"

"Excuse me? My name is Katherine James and this is my house. How may I help you?"

"You can bring Ella to the door before all hell breaks loose."

"Ella? She's not here. She left to marry my son, Ken."

"Not a fucking chance," Shelly fumes. "This cunt is lying. Ken makes Ella's skin crawl."

"Not to mention that she's already engaged to me," I tell the woman glaring at us.

"Hey. What's that noise?" Jeremy asks. We all listen for a moment.

"It's Cujo!" Shelly and I say in unison.

"Ella left him here so she and Ken could have some alone time."

"No way. She never leaves him here when she's gone. She always brings him to me or my mom because she doesn't trust either one of them with him," Shelly spouts back.

"Look, lady. You'd better back the fuck up and let us in," I push her aside as I storm in, wild eyed, looking for my princess. "Ella! Ella, where are you, baby?"

"What's going on?" a slimy looking fucker says while walking in.

"Ken, I presume? Funny. I thought you and Ella were off getting married."

"Um, yeah. I just came back for a second. She's at the courthouse, waiting for me."

That's when I lose it. "Bullshit! You'd better tell me where she is right this second or you are a dead man." I slam him against the wall, crushing his windpipe with my arm.

"I'm calling the police!" Katherine yells.

"That's great. Tell the chief I said hi."

I start choking Ken. He claws at my hands. I let him go for a moment. "Okay, okay. She's in the dungeon."

"Where the hell is that? Take me to it. Jeremy, watch the bitch. Ella had better be unharmed or neither of you will live to see another day."

Fifty-Seven

Ella

Someone is coming. I look around for weapons, but find nothing. The door bursts open. "Prince!" I fling my arms around him, crying because I'm so relieved. "I can't believe you found me!"

"I'll always find you, baby. No take backs. Remember?"

"I remember." I smile, then kiss him for all I'm worth. Cujo jumps against his leg, interrupting us.

"And this must be the killer dog I've heard so much about. He seems harmless enough." He picks up Cujo, who covers his face with kisses.

"Holy crap! He actually likes you."

"What's not to like?"

"Prince, you don't understand. He only likes me. There are a few people that he tolerates, and everyone else he hates."

"Maybe he's just a really good judge of character," he smirks.

"Could be."

"Move!" Ken yells. We turn around to see him pointing a gun at us.

"What exactly is your plan here, Ken?" Prince asks calmly, setting Cujo down.

"She and I are getting married," he says, pointing at me. I feel bile rise in my throat at the thought of it.

"Over my dead body," Prince growls.

"That can be arranged," Ken says, cocking the gun and aiming it directly at him.

"Wait! I'll go; just don't hurt him."

"Princess…" he growls again.

"It's okay, Prince. We'll find a way out of this."

Ken lowers the gun and motions for me to walk in front of him. As he starts to turn, all hell breaks loose. Shelly comes in and whacks him over the head with a brick, just as Cujo sinks his teeth into his leg. Ken squeals in pain, dropping the gun and falling to the floor. Prince punches him in the nose, spewing blood everywhere.

Within minutes, Jeremy and Prince manage to tie up Ken and Katherine. As we wait for the police, Prince holds me close, stroking my back. "You are safe now, Princess."

Fifty-Eight

Prince

I can't believe how close I came to losing Ella. If I hadn't come back early from my trip, I don't know what would have happened. I don't even want to think about it. It may be awhile before I am comfortable letting her out of my sight. I hold her and Cujo close as we answer the police's questions.

Once they tell Katherine and Ken that they are going to jail, they can't rat each other out fast enough. It turns out they really are evil. They killed Ella's dad to get his money, only to find out that it all went to Ella. They had only kept her alive so that she and Ken could marry once she turned twenty-one, per the terms of the will; then they would kill her, too, and have all of the money.

On top of everything else, they weren't even mother and son; they were lovers. I don't even want to think about that. They deserve everything that is coming to them.

"So they killed my father?" Ella asks with tears streaming down her face. She loved him very much, and her time with him was cut short because of these two.

"I'm so sorry, baby." I rock her gently, trying to comfort her.

Ella's inheritance would go directly to her if she married, so they figured they would force her to marry Ken, then forge a will leaving everything to the two of them before she had a tragic accident. It's a good thing I came along when I did.

Ella looks so stunned. Poor baby. She has always called Katherine her evil stepmother. That might have been an understatement.

The police finally finish up and take them away. They will both be going away for a long, long time. "What an awful day," Ella sniffs.

"I know, baby. I'm so sorry. How about we make up for it by making tomorrow a perfect day?" I ask as I kiss the top of her head.

She finally smiles. "What did you have in mind?"

Fifty-Nine

Ella

What he had in mind was a whirlwind wedding. Not only that, Shelly and Jeremy are getting married, too. My bestie and I are having a double wedding! I have no idea how that came about, but I can't wait to find out. I've never seen her so happy.

Prince has done everything possible to make it the wedding of my dreams. He even had the sweet lady from *Your Fairy Godmother* bring me a gorgeous wedding dress. I have no idea how he pulled everything together so fast. All that matters is that we are together, along with a few other people, and (of course!) Cujo. He's our ring bearer, dressed in an adorable doggy tuxedo.

Shelly and I finish fixing each others veils, trying not to cry. "Can you believe this? We were both single just a few days ago."

She laughs. "I know. We both landed the men of our dreams at a fairy tale ball. How cool is that? Maybe our fairy godmother really knew what she was talking about."

Her mom pops her head in. "Are you ladies ready?"

We squeeze each other's hands. "Absolutely!"

Sixty

Prince

Ella walks down the aisle toward me. I am transfixed by her beauty. Much like her gown for the ball, this one shimmers and seems to almost glow. It is gorgeous, but nowhere near as stunning as my princess.

"You are so beautiful," I whisper against her lips.

"Thank you." I kiss her again.

The minister clears his throat. "If I may. Dearly beloved…"

The ceremony goes by in a flash. I repeat my vows, never taking my eyes off of Ella. I don't know how I ever got so lucky, but I'm never letting her go.

When it comes time to kiss my bride, I probably earn an R rating with my kiss. I take her lips hungrily, over and over, until I hear someone say, "Jeez. Get a room." We both laugh. I pick her up bridal style, and rush her back down the aisle, and toward the hotel's honeymoon suite. I can't claim my bride fast enough.

Sixty-One

Prince

"Prince, you can put me down now, you know."

"Not until I've carried you over the threshold of our room." I carry her through the living area and deposit her on a very large bed covered in rose petals.

"Oh, Prince! This is so beautiful! I love it!"

"Anything for you, my love." It feels like deja vu as I strip my tuxedo off so that I can ravish my bride.

"Don't even think about tearing this dress off of me, Prince. There's a zipper hidden on the side that you can use instead."

"Good thing. I only have so much self control, princess."

"It's one of the things I love most about you."

"Let me give you a demonstration." I carefully unzip and strip away her dress, leaving her in the sexiest lingerie I've ever seen. It's a white lace confection that pushes her breasts up while emphasizing her tiny waist and wide hips. She has garter belts on, completing the sexy look. My cock immediately turns to stone.

"Fuck me, angel. You look stunning. Good enough to eat."

"Funny. I was hoping you would say that." I take her mouth with all the hunger that I'm feeling.

"You look so beautiful in this, sweetheart, but you'll look even better out of it." I pull her bra down, revealing her juicy tits. I take time to suck and kiss each one. I squeeze her plump breasts in my hands and lavish attention on them.

I work my way down her body, taking her lingerie off as I go. I kiss along her thighs as I take off her garters. I'm worked up now and running out of patience. I tear her panties off, reveling in how damp they are.

"So wet for me, baby." She throws her head back as I stroke her pussy lips and push a finger inside.

"Oh, god, Prince. That feels so good."

"Just wait, princess." With that, I push her back onto the bed and devour her drenched cunt, while my fist squeezes the hell out of my cock to stop it from going off. I suck hard on her clit, making her scream. Her release immediately gushes against my face. "So fucking sexy, baby."

I climb on top of her, slamming all the way into her sweetness with one thrust. We both moan our pleasure. I try to go slow, but she feels too good. Before long, I am slamming inside her as hard as I can while she raises her hips up to meet my thrusts. She comes again, crying out my name. Her tight little pussy clamps down hard, sending me over the edge.

I gather her against me and pull the covers over us. I kiss her gently. "Happy wedding day, Mrs. Sterling."

She smiles at me. "Happy wedding day, Mr. Sterling."

Sixty-Two

Epilogue–Ella

The last two months have been insanely busy. I put the castle on the market. The bad memories outweighed the good, so I didn't have any desire to hang onto it. I'm now in control of all of my inheritance. I decided to open an animal shelter, so Prince has been helping me with all the logistics. I'm so excited!

We found a house that we love out in the country. It is perfect for a growing family. It's a beautiful country estate, but it looks like a home; warm and welcoming. We just moved in a few days ago. We had been staying at Prince's family estate, along with his parents. It's a very nice house, but we are newlyweds and seriously need our privacy. I think Mrs. Sterling walking in on us going at it in Prince's home office was the last straw. Prince decided we needed our own place where he could fuck me anytime and anywhere he wanted. I couldn't agree more.

Cujo has happily settled into his new digs. He has become much friendlier to everyone. Maybe he knew that Katherine and Ken were evil and was just in protective mode all the time. Who knows.

He continues to be Prince's biggest fan, besides me, of course. He happily snuggles up with us both in the bed and on the couch. I've been thinking about adopting another rescue dog so he will have a friend to play with twenty-four seven. I just need to talk to Prince about it first. Knowing him, he will say yes. He lives to make me happy. He has been beyond my wildest dreams.

Speaking of, I hear him pull into the garage. "Princess, I'm home."

"Hi, baby," I race to him and am immediately picked up and kissed within an inch of my life. "Goodness. What a greeting!"

"I can't help it. I've missed you. I like when you go to the office with me. I hate when you stay home. How would you feel about me working from home a few days a week?"

"Oh, Prince. I would love it!" Cujo barks his agreement and spins in circles, demonstrating his approval. He sends us into gales of laughter.

"I brought your favorite for dinner; shrimp scampi." He brings out the bag, but one whiff has me racing toward the bathroom and emptying the contents of my stomach. "Sweetheart, are you okay?"

"I don't know what's wrong with me. I must have a bug. I don't think I can eat the shrimp scampi. For some reason, the smell is really grossing me out."

"That's okay, sweetheart. I'll get you whatever you want," he says as he helps me rinse my mouth with mouthwash.

The next morning, I bolt out of bed, barely making it to the bathroom in time to toss my cookies again. I feel like shit. I don't know what my problem is. Prince calmly hands me mouthwash, and runs a cool washcloth over my face before helping me back to bed.

"I'm kind of shocked you are taking this so well. I'm surprised you haven't brought in a team of specialists to see what's wrong with me."

He smiles. "I know you feel terrible, princess, but I'm pretty sure it's because you have a little one growing inside you."

"What? Oh my gosh! I've been so busy with everything, that never even crossed my mind."

He kisses my forehead. "It's been on my mind since the moment I first laid eyes on you. We've got an appointment with a specialist this afternoon. Just rest until then."

A few hours later, we confirm what Prince suspected. I am indeed pregnant. It looks like I may have even gotten pregnant the night of the ball. We both cry tears of happiness. This is just the beginning of our happily ever after.

THE END

If you enjoyed these stories, please take a few moments to write a review of them. Thank you!

*More books in the Twisted Sexy Fairy Tales and Obsessed Alphas series will be coming up soon. If you want to read Shelly and Jeremy's story, pick up **Seducing Shelly.***

About the Author

Lacy Jane is a happily married empty nester and dog mom who believes in happily ever afters and loves to write about them. She enjoys reading steamy romances, streaming shows, and watching football and baseball. She loves hanging out with her husband, kids, friends, family, and dogs. She loves traveling, shopping, drinking delicious coffee drinks, and is a self-professed beauty junkie. Her books are always OTT, high heat, instalove, no cheating, and (of course!) have an HEA.Always a steamy read with HEA guaranteed.

You can connect with me on:

https://lacy-jane.mailchimpsites.com

Subscribe to my newsletter:

https://lacy-jane.mailchimpsites.com

My books are always OTT, and contain instalove, high heat, no cheating, and (of course!) a HEA. Always a steamy read with HEA guaranteed. Enjoy!

Seducing Shelly (An OTT Steamy Age Gap Office Romance): Obsessed Alphas Book 4
You met Jeremy and Shelly in Enticing Ella. Now you can read their steamy love story.

Jeremy
Shelly is smart.
She's beautiful.
She's perfect.
She's also my assistant, so she is totally off limits to me.
How can I keep my hands to myself when she's everything I've ever wanted?

Shelly
Jeremy is a hot, older man.
He's the sexiest guy I've ever seen.
He's also my boss, and way out of my league.
How can I stay professional when all I can think about is him?

See what happens when Shelly and Jeremy give in to their undeniable attraction.

This book is an OTT instalove with high heat, no cheating, and (of course!) a HEA. A steamy read with HEA guaranteed. Enjoy!

Claiming Callie (An OTT, Age Gap, Dad's Best Friend Steamy Romance): Obsessed Alphas Book 5

Callie

> *Rex Cameron, aka Uncle Rex.*
> *Former NFL tight end.*
> *Six-foot-eight of mouthwatering muscles.*
> *Star of my naughtiest fantasies.*
> *The only man I've ever wanted.*

Dad's best friend, so totally off limits.

Rex

> *Callie Stevens.*
> *John's little girl.*
> *Sexiest woman to ever walk the face of the earth.*
> *Pin-up worthy curves and f*ck me eyes.*
> *The object of my every dirty desire.*
> *I'm twice her age.*
> *She's like family to me.*
> *She's forbidden fruit.*
> *She's all I can think about.*
> *Once I touch her, all bets are off.*
> *Once I claim her, I'll never let her go.*

A sexy older man, a beautiful younger woman, and a forbidden romance. This book is OTT with light daddy/lg elements, _very_ high heat, no cheating, and (of course!) a HEA. If you prefer your romances squeaky clean, this is not the book for you. If, on the other hand, you like lots of sex, dirty talking heroes, and strong heroines who know what they want, read away! A steamy read with HEA guaranteed. Enjoy!

Seducing Her Stalker (A safe stalker, steamy, age gap romance): (Obsessed Alphas Book 3)

Can a stalker find happiness with the object of his obsession?

From the moment Jaxon sees Serena, he becomes completely obsessed with her. His life suddenly revolves around the sweet, sexy librarian. He finds himself crossing more and more lines as his obsession intensifies. When he finds out she returns his feelings, he is determined to make her his. Will she still feel the same if she finds out how deep his obsession with her is?

Like all of my books, this is an OTT instalove with high heat, no cheating, and (of course!) a HEA. If you are looking for a squeaky clean romance, I am not your girl. If you like your romance a little on the dirty side, read away! Always a steamy read with HEA guaranteed. Enjoy!

Seduced by the Witness: (Obsessed Alphas-Book 1)
When a sexy FBI agent and a curvy, gorgeous witness are thrown together, sparks fly. Can they resist each other, or will they give in to their desires? Find out in this steamy, close proximity romance.

This book has instalove, high heat, no cheating, and (of course!) a HEA. My books are for those who like their happily ever after a little on the dirty side. Always a steamy read with HEA guaranteed. Enjoy!

Seducing My Wife: (Obsessed Alphas Book 2)
Can Jace convince Chloe to give him a second chance? Find out if this very passionate couple can resolve their differences in this quick, steamy read.

This book is high heat, no cheating, instalove, and (of course!) a HEA. My books are for those who like their happily ever after a little on the dirty side. Always a steamy read with HEA guaranteed. Enjoy!